"Images of mermaids swim throughout *How to Love a Jamaican*, Alexia Arthurs's shimmering story collection. . . . With its singular mix of psychological precision and sun-kissed lyricism, this dazzling debut marks the emergence of a knockout new voice."
—O: *The Oprah Magazine*

"In this book, there's no single way to be Jamaican—the definition of the word itself expands to encompass each person who claims it."
—*The Paris Review*

"Arthurs complicates the very idea of a unifying national identity. She paints a disparate but not disjointed portrait of a complex national and diasporic landscape. To love any one Jamaican, Arthurs implies, you must first *learn* them."
—*The Atlantic*

"Explores subjects ranging from identity and what it means to be a woman, to heritage and what it means to be Jamaican."
—*Vanity Fair*

"Arthurs's debut is vivid and exciting, and every story rings beautifully true."
—*Marie Claire*

"A sublime short story collection from newcomer Alexia Arthurs that explores, through various characters, a specific strand of the immigrant experience. Though this is the author's first book, the prose is assured and textured, enlivened by a personal touch—Arthurs's own life, growing up and living as an undocumented immigrant in the U.S. until the age of twenty-four."
—*Entertainment Weekly*

"This collection is brimming with tenderness, hard realities, and an intimacy that will stay with you long after you've turned the last page."
—AYANA MATHIS, author of
The Twelve Tribes of Hattie

"Alexia Arthurs is a voice so many of us have been waiting for—funny, achingly specific and wonderfully universal. She explores what it means to belong, what it means to recognize yourself in the most unexpected places, and what humans do with the pain of longing." —KAITLYN GREENIDGE, author of *We Love You, Charlie Freeman*

"What a thrill to recognize myself and the women I love in Alexia Arthurs's stunning debut story collection. This fantastic young writer conjures the fierce wit of Jamaica Kincaid and the deft storytelling of Chimamanda Ngozi Adichie. . . . Entrancing and unforgettable." —NAOMI JACKSON, author of *The Star Side of Bird Hill*

"The stories hum with tension and nuance, creating characters desperate to be understood but wary of being defined simply by their race or origins." —Associated Press

"I give this book an A+." —BILL GOLDSTEIN on "Bill's Books," NBC New York

"In her riveting debut collection of short stories, Alexia Arthurs explores a vast range of issues, from race and class to gender and family. A Jamaican immigrant who moved to Brooklyn at the impressionable age of twelve, she tells vivid stories that keep readers on their toes." —*Essence*

"Alexia Arthurs's debut, *How to Love a Jamaican*, is equal parts relatable and thought-provoking, providing an in-depth look at how much living within and outside of borders dictates who we are." —*Shondaland*

"Arthurs's debut collection of short stories is an impressive, fully realized work that grapples with Jamaican womanhood. . . . Arthurs offers a compassionate response with these tender portraits of hard women, lost girls, and the people who love them." —*The Village Voice*

"In vibrant, evocative prose, Arthurs brings these characters, and their varied experiences of a shared home, to life."
—*Buzzfeed* ("30 Summer Books to Get Excited About")

"These stories unravel the knot of being in a place but not quite belonging and the sense of missing but not quite understanding what was lost. . . . This strong debut collection . . . beckons the reader back, again and again. . . . A lovely collection of stories that rewards subsequent readings."
—*Kirkus Reviews*

"Perpetually engaging . . . While the stories have a rawness to them, exploring topics such as sexual orientation, parental relationships, self-discovery, and drug use, Arthurs also offers a sure feel of the mysticism of the Caribbean. . . . Stylistically reminiscent of Toni Morrison's *Paradise*, this successful debut will appeal to readers of literary and Caribbean fiction."
—*Library Journal*

"A vibrant, wrenching, and expansive short story collection that illuminates the nuances of the immigrant experience."
—*Bustle*

"The latest in a wave of vital fiction about the immigrant experience."
—*Newsday*

How to Love a Jamaican

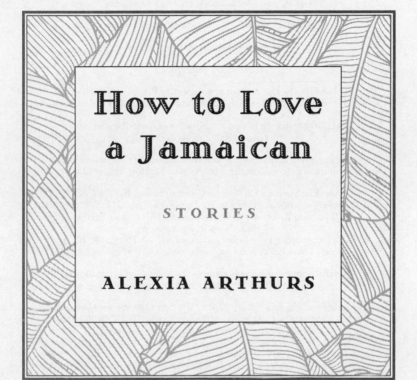

How to Love a Jamaican

STORIES

ALEXIA ARTHURS

BALLANTINE BOOKS

NEW YORK

2019 Ballantine Books Trade Paperback Edition

Published in the United States by Ballantine Books, an imprint of Random House, a division of Penguin Random House LLC, New York.

BALLANTINE and the HOUSE colophon are registered trademarks of Penguin Random House LLC.

Originally published in hardcover in the United States by Ballantine Books, an imprint of Random House, a division of Penguin Random House LLC, in 2018.

"Slack" was first published in *Virginia Quarterly Review* (no. 94.1 Fall 2017). "Bad Behavior" was first published in *The Paris Review* (no. 217, Summer 2016). "Mermaid River" was first published in *The Sewanee Review* (vol. CXXVI, no. 2, Spring 2018). "The Ghost of Jia Yi" was first published in *Vice* (December 2017). "Shirley from a Small Place" was first published in *Granta* online (Spring 2018).

Grateful acknowledgment is made to the following for permission to reprint previously published material:

Carcanet Press Limited: Excerpt from "The Law Concerning Mermaids" from *A Light Song of Light* by Kei Miller, copyright © 2010 by Kei Miller. Reprinted by permission of Carcanet Press Limited. W. W. Norton & Company, Inc.: Excerpt from "From the House of Yemanjá" from *The Collected Poems of Audre Lorde* by Audre Lorde, copyright © 1997 by The Audre Lorde Estate. Reprinted by permission of W. W. Norton & Company, Inc.

LIBRARY OF CONGRESS CATALOGING-IN-PUBLICATION DATA
Names: Arthurs, Alexia author.
Title: How to love a Jamaican: stories / Alexia Arthurs.
Description: First edition. | New York: Ballantine Books, 2018.
Identifiers: LCCN 2018006289 | ISBN 9781524799229 |
ISBN 9781524799212 (ebook)
Subjects: LCSH: Jamaicans—Fiction. | Jamaican Americans—Fiction.
Classification: LCC PS3601.R764 A6 2018 | DDC 813/.6—dc23 LC
record available at https://lccn.loc.gov/2018006289

Printed in the United States of America on acid-free paper

randomhousebooks.com

9 8 7 6 5 4 3 2 1

Book design by Jo Anne Metsch

FOR JAMAICANS

And maybe this is the problem with empires: how they have forced us to live in a world lacking in mermaids—mermaids who understood that they simply were, and did not need permission to exist or to be beautiful.

—KEI MILLER, "The Law Concerning Mermaids"

CONTENTS

How to Love a Jamaican

LIGHT-SKINNED GIRLS
AND KELLY ROWLANDS

The first time I saw Cecilia, she was the only other black girl in our small group during freshman orientation. We were sitting in a circle while the junior leading our group was answering questions anyone had, and then we each had to say our name and where we were from. When it came to Cecilia's turn, I had already memorized her name from the nametag, and carefully, without bringing attention to myself, took her in: flawless dark skin, silky relaxed hair that reached her breasts, tall, thin, beautiful. In that song "Power," when Kanye West raps, "Ma'fucka', we rollin' with some light-skinned girls and some Kelly Rowlands," he is talking about dark-skinned girls who look like Cecilia. But Cecilia isn't the kind of name that brings to mind a black girl, and that day when she spoke, telling us that she was from California, her voice reminded me of all those blonde white girls on reality television, confirming that, as I suspected, she was a white girl trapped in a black girl's body—an Oreo. I could forgive her for this, as I was crowned an Oreo in high school because I liked spending my free period with my hands in clay in the ceramics classroom and I liked listening to the kind of music played in coffee shops in the city.

But then I could tell that Cecilia was an Oreo who really might have forgotten the color of her skin, because when the group was dismissed, I walked up to her to ask which part of California she was from. This was the only question I could think to ask her. "The Bay Area," she told me, and it was clear that she wasn't particularly interested in me, that although we were black women, that was neither here nor there. I might as well have been talking to a white boy. Up until that moment, all of my experiences with black people in a sea of white faces was that we acknowledged each other, whether it was by eye contact or a smile, and that we would eventually make it across the room to each other. We might have been invisible to everyone else but we weren't invisible to each other. That day, Cecilia left the orientation room with a white girl, the both of them cracking up at what seemed to be the funniest joke of the year. I'd overheard the white girl introduce Cecilia to someone as her roommate.

When I tell my mother that Cecilia and I are no longer friends, she doesn't lift her face from her Facebook account. My mother only recently discovered social media, and is obsessed because it allows her to reacquaint herself with people she knew back in Jamaica. "You and her will mek up back," she tells me, with such conviction that for a moment I believe her. When I am walking out of the living room, she says, "You know dis site nuh easy? It just encourage people fi fass inna people business." I don't respond to her, but I almost smile.

The thing about attending university in New York City is that so many of my classmates think that New York is heaven, or close enough, or maybe it's hell depending on how you see things. But to me, it's home. My first year, I overheard my classmates' excitement about the city, the things they had done, the people they had slept with, and when I wasn't rolling my eyes, I envied that they were having more fun than me. My mother couldn't afford to pay for the dormitory and a loan was out of the question since I lived an hour away, so I went to my classes and then I went home.

I met Cecilia for the second time during our sophomore year. I'd seen her around a few times, but each time she didn't seem to remember meeting me. She was always with some little white girl, all of them in crop tops and the other dumb clothes hipsters wear. One time I saw her holding hands with a white boy, who was a little bit handsome when I crossed my eyes, but mostly ugly. He had the hipster look to him, greasy long hair and a beard, like he might write poetry or song lyrics. Probably an English major. God, I'd hate to be in his fiction workshop. I could tell he'd had a middle-class upbringing from a place like the Bay Area. You know, I don't think I've met a person from the Bay Area who I liked. His parents would be glad to know that their son had moved to New York and taken up with a black girl. They would call her "beautiful" even if she wasn't. See, if I'm going to date a white man, he has to be sexy, he has to have the swag of a black man, like Justin Timberlake. Otherwise, why bother?

That spring semester, I was surprised to see that Cecilia was in my photography class. She ignored me until halfway into the semester, when we hung up our portrait projects on the wall and the teacher liked mine best. With everyone else he was in teacher mode, giving the obligatory compliments and suggestions, but with mine he stood in front of my photos for longer than he had with the others, and then he asked, "Is this your first photography class, Kimberly?" I'd taken photographs of four of the women who live on my block. I didn't ask any of the men because it would have been more awkward to ask them. Plus, half of them always have a fresh look on their face when I walk past in my tight jeans. One of the photographs was of my mother. It was Sunday morning and because my mother belongs to the religion of obsessive cleaning, she was sweeping outside of the house we share with two other families. When I approached with my camera, she kissed her teeth, complaining that I was bothering her. Didn't I see that she had on her housedress and rollers in her hair? Of course I saw, but I wanted to take natural photographs. In my favorite photographs, the people are as beautiful or as unbeautiful as they really are, their faces caught in an emotion that reminds you that life is a whole lot of feeling. I tried to explain that the rollers and the broom added character, which made my mother laugh, and it was while she was laughing that I started taking photographs. I also took photographs of the old women across the street. In the afternoon, one of them goes to the other one's porch, which is where they sit, sometimes talking, other times just looking into the street as if the streets in Canarsie are pretty to look at (they aren't), until it's time to make their husbands' dinners. My mother, because she's paranoid, says that they sit there talking people's business, but I hope it's more interesting than that. I asked if I could take their photograph, and they looked doubtful until I said it was for school. "When pickney want fi better demself yuh ha' fi support dem," Mrs. Patterson said, and it was clear by how Mrs. Johnson nodded that she was speaking for the both of them. In the photos I took, the lines in their faces were illuminated, telling of the places they'd been and the people they'd seen. My last subject was the fat white woman who lives in the house next to us. Her name is Sheryl, and she has big, hanging breasts under her housedress. She always wears a housedress and never a bra. When she's walking her small furry dog, if my mother is outside, she'll stop and talk to her, as lively as though they are friends. Mostly what she tells my mother is gossip. Apparently, the Haitian family that lives down the street hasn't paid rent in three months. Sheryl's breasts fascinate me, and meanwhile my mother is saying, "Oh wow," which is what she says when she wishes someone, especially a white someone, would stop talking. When Sheryl leaves, my mother will sigh dramatically, and say, "Then what I do fi dat woman harass me?" The day I photographed Sheryl, I asked her permission, but I expected to hear no because who would want photographs taken with their breasts hanging heavy and low? "Take me and Coco," Sheryl said, lifting the dog to her face. Behind us, I could tell that my mother wanted to burst out laughing. When Sheryl left, my mother shook her head and said, "White people tek crazy to a whole oda level. Yuh know I haven't prayed inna long time? Tonight mi a get down pon mi knees fi dat woman."

After that photography class, I saw Cecilia in Trader Joe's. I was there for various cookies and other sweet treats my mother and I eye in our kitchen and say encouraging things about, like "Oh, three of them are only 120 calories" and "I'm not going to have any more tonight." Cecilia only had two bottles of sparkling water in her hands, while I had a jar of cookie butter and three kinds of cookies. She was standing by the meat section as though she was waiting for someone.

"Hi," she said when I walked by pretending not to notice her. She was smiling as though she was glad to see me. I almost looked behind me to see if she was talking to someone else.

"Hi?" I asked her.

"Kimberly, right?"

"Right."

"Cecilia."

"We've met before. Remember, during freshman orientation?"

"Oh yeah," she said, but I couldn't tell if she remembered meeting me. When you're invisible to a white person, you can almost get used to that. But when it's a black person, you can't help feeling hurt.

"Those portraits you took were so beautiful," Cecilia said.

"Oh, wow, thank you," I told her, annoyed that a compliment from her meant so much to me.

"They reminded me of Gordon Parks's work."

"Are you serious? That's, like, the best compliment ever."

"Is photography your major?"

"Maybe. Or I might major in fine arts. You?"

"I want to do something creative, but I don't know what yet. I might want to be a writer, but I don't know if I'm any good. My boyfriend is majoring in creative writing and he says that I'm better than any of the people he's had classes with, but I don't know."

"Oh," I said, pleased that I was right about her boyfriend. I wonder if white people are as good at reading us. Probably not. We've spent our whole lives observing them. It makes sense that we'd be good at it.

"Well, there's my boyfriend."

I turned around to see the same guy I'd seen with her before.

"This is Kimberly," Cecilia said, motioning toward me.

"I'm Adam," he said, smiling in the way nice white men smile. "I'd shake your hand if my hands weren't filled." He was holding two jars of peanut butter, a bag of apples, and a loaf of bread.

"Kimberly is the most talented person in our photography class," Cecilia said. This made Adam look at me with renewed interest.

"Oh really," he said. "Where are you from?"

"I'm from here," I said.

"It must have been amazing to grow up in New York."

"It was all right," I said, smiling and shrugging.

"Come on! All right?"

"Where are you from?"

"Born and raised in Denver."

"Are there any black people in Denver?"

"A few." He laughed. "Yeah, it would have been nice to grow up in a place as diverse as New York. Have you always lived here?"

"No, actually my mother and I moved here from Jamaica when I was six."

"You're Jamaican?" Cecilia asked, visibly surprised.

"Yeah. Why are you surprised?"

"Because I'm Jamaican. Well, I wasn't born there but it's where both my parents are from."

"Really?"

"Why are *you* so surprised?"

"Oh," I said, grasping for a convincing excuse. "It's just an unexpected coincidence."

They left soon after, Cecilia saying that we should get coffee. I'd only smiled, instead of agreeing with her.

The next time we had class together, Cecilia came up to me afterwards, asking if I was free and whether I was hungry. "I can eat," I told her, careful not to sound too eager. Usually, when I wanted a sandwich, I went to a bodega for a cheap, tasty turkey sandwich that was so big I could leave the rest for another meal. The place Cecilia took me to was one of those bougie sandwich shops that also serve soup, salad, and little, uppity bags of potato chips. I paid almost ten dollars for a turkey sandwich that was quite good, but then I couldn't afford a drink and a bag of potato chips like if I'd gone to a bodega in Brooklyn. Cecilia, who had claimed to be "*so hungry*," ordered a bowl of soup that came with a little packet of oyster crackers. I looked at the small bowl of thick soup with a few chunks of beef and vegetables and asked her again if it really cost seven dollars.

"Which dorm do you live in?" Cecilia asked me.

"I actually live at home with my mother. It didn't make any sense to pay all that money to live in a dorm."

"But then you don't get the full college experience!"

"I know, but I'll survive. Maybe I'll go away for graduate school."

"How's living with your mother?"

"She's annoying in all the ways mothers are annoying. But we're really close, since I didn't grow up with my father."

"I couldn't wait to get away from my mother. My father is okay, but my mother is so involved. Both my parents are professors, which maybe explains why my mother has such ambitions for me, but Jesus Christ."

"What do you mean by 'ambitions'?"

"I feel like my mother planned out my life and all she wanted was for me to agree, and when I didn't agree, it was as though I'd disappointed her."

"Do you think it's because your mother is Jamaican? Caribbean mothers want to eat their daughters."

"Eat?" Cecilia asked, laughing. "That's a funny way of putting it. I wonder that sometimes, especially when my mother talks about her mother. The first time my mother brought my father home and my grandmother saw how dark he was, she barely looked at him. She disliked him and she could never give my mother a concrete reason why. My mother would speak so badly about her mother, but then when she died I don't think anyone cried more at the funeral."

"It was the same way with my mother. My grandma almost kicked her out of the house when she became pregnant with me. My mother will speak about her mother as though she was this horrible person, I mean like the biggest bitch in the world, but then once in a while she'll get all sentimental and say that my grandma was a God-fearing woman. It's weird."

After that lunch date, Cecilia and I became friends. I don't know the exact moment we turned to each other the way flowers turn toward the sun. If life was a film, the music would have slowed and our eyes would have softened, but real-life moments, however crucial, can be so subtle that sometimes we hardly notice how, as people say, the chips have fallen. We became less available to others in the way that some people forget other relationships when they fall in love. I don't know why more love stories aren't written about platonic intimacy. My close girlfriends, relationships forged back in high school, were the daughters of Caribbean immigrants, and they had left me lonely when we separated to attend different colleges. In college I'd met people I studied with and hung out with on occasion, but I hadn't really had a bosom friend till Cecilia.

Eventually I took her home with me, to a version of New York she may never have seen her entire four years at school in the city. To a girl like that, there was no reason to take the L train to the very last stop in Brooklyn—instead, she might take the L train from the city a few stops into Brooklyn for vegan ice cream in a gentrified neighborhood. I explained that Canarsie, the neighborhood that surrounded the last stop of the L train, used to be filled with white people until, according to my mother, the black people drove them out, not on purpose but just by being black. I told Cecilia that there were three Jamaican families on my block, and almost every other family was from another Caribbean island. And for Cecilia's part, she invited me into her social group, and then I was interacting with the kinds of people, particularly white people, I'd sit next to in classes but never really hang out with. I even let Adam's friend, Ryan, make out with me one night when we'd drunk too much wine and he offered to walk me to the train station. When he'd kissed me before I walked down the stairs to catch the L train, it reminded me of the kind of thing I would see in a movie set in New York City. Snowflakes were falling gently from the sky, and it was the kind of winter day that was comfortably cold. Moments like those, New York opens itself up, surprises me, whispers its secrets to me, even calls me by name, and I am left believing that the city really is as magical as people are always saying. He'd put his hand on my face and looked into my eyes, both of which a man had never done with me before. When a man looks at you like that, it's easy to believe that you're beautiful, which is why I smiled the whole train ride home.

. . .

The first time New York opened up for me was when I was fifteen and spending the summer participating in an arts program at Stuyvesant High School. I was in the Visual Arts track, and when all the tracks came together to eat lunch, I noticed two black guys sitting a table away. Later I would learn that they were brothers who lived in the Bronx. My closest friend in my track was a Dominican boy named José, who called me "girl"—as in, "Girl, that painting is looking fierce." On the first day, we'd introduced ourselves by saying our name and which high school we went to, and when I said that I was a rising junior at John Dewey in Brooklyn, José interrupted, excited to say that that's where his cousin went. Afterwards, he came up to me to ask if I knew his cousin. I didn't know her, but when he showed me a photograph on his phone I recognized her because she'd fought another girl on the train, the both of them pulling each other's hair and throwing punches. The train car had been packed with onlookers and instigators from our high school crowding around the two of them. Eventually, when José's cousin reached to the back of her own head and looked at the wad of hair in her hand, she'd started to cry and got off the train at the next stop, which meant that the other girl, a brolic type everyone said was bisexual, had won. I didn't know how to say all of this to José—that I'd seen his cousin beaten and crying—so I said that I'd never seen her before. After that, he worked next to me in the studio, and at lunch he sat next to me.

One day that summer, José asked if I would deliver a note

for him. He motioned to one of the black brothers, explaining that a note was his way of pursuing Malik. "Wait, how do you even know he's gay?" I asked. José only laughed. I delivered the note and immediately José and Malik were lovers, holding hands as we walked in the West Village in the afternoons after classes, along with Malik's younger brother Maurice, who everyone called Baby. We were sidekicks, Baby and myself. I was disappointed to discover that Baby was bisexual, because once when he'd held my hand and looked very carefully at my fingers to see how badly I'd bitten my nails I'd felt shy, but I was intimidated and turned off by the fact that he was also interested in men. When I really thought about it, I was a Jamaican girl entirely out of my comfort zone.

Malik and Baby took us to where they lived in the Bronx. I'd never been anywhere like that before—the bathroom and kitchen surfaces were overrun with baby cockroaches, the smell of pee sliced the air, and the little grandmother paid us no mind because she was too old, too far gone, to notice us. There were the nieces, two chatty little girls with hair badly in need of combing. I watched one of them smash a baby cockroach between her fingers, and I looked around quickly for some kind of explanation and commiseration, but Malik and José were behind a closed door and Baby was watching a daytime talk show with his grandmother.

Another time, on our way to where Malik and Baby lived, we bumped into their sister a few blocks from the apartment. She was braless under a white T-shirt and with a man who had a large scar across one of his cheeks. I was afraid because

I'd never been around drug addicts before. Later, in the apartment, amidst the baby cockroaches, the sleeping old woman, and the little girls playing with Barbie dolls on the dirty floor, Malik and Baby showed José and me a new dance they'd taught themselves. They danced to a Britney Spears song in the kitchen, and for reasons I didn't quite understand, they'd incorporated knives—big shiny ones that looked out of place in that dilapidated apartment—into the routine. One slip and someone would have to call my mother. But Malik and Baby held tight, they danced and lip-synched, and I watched with some astonishment, thinking about how much larger and diverse the world and its people were than I had realized. We all stayed friends till the end of summer.

The next time I saw Cecilia, she was excited when she asked about the walk to the subway with Ryan. "He's a nice guy," I said, wondering if Ryan had spilled that we'd kissed. I hadn't planned to tell her about the kiss, because she would have made it into more than it was. "I think he really likes you," she told me.

It seemed clear that Cecilia was the kind of black girl who didn't think about her race as much as I did. It seemed to me that the world wouldn't let me forget. This was why I couldn't help rolling my eyes when Cecilia said something like "I just love blue-eyed men." "You should read *The Bluest Eye*," I'd challenged her. "I've read it," she said, looking annoyed. "Toni Morrison is a goddess," she added. I'd read that book the semester before, and it explained so many of the stories black women tell themselves. I didn't understand how Cecilia could say that she liked blue eyes as though there wasn't anything to liking blue eyes. As if blue eyes were an innocent desire for a black woman.

Adam broke up with Cecilia around the time we'd started hanging out, which was probably one of the reasons we'd gotten close. She had more time to invest in her relationships with women and she liked hearing that I thought she could do better than Adam. I observed that every man she pointed to in school or around the city, men she joked about rebounding with, were all white.

"You seem to like white men," I told her.

"I like all men. Somehow, I've managed to keep my inner ho restrained," she said, smiling.

"But you seem to especially like white men."

"That's not true at all."

One time we got into a mini-argument because Cecilia thought it was hypocritical for black women like me to say that we prefer black men but then judge black women who prefer white men.

"What's the difference?" she asked, and I was so surprised that for a moment I only stood there shaking my head.

Then I said, "When it comes to race relations, the white man is the single most oppressive entity in the world, and you're asking me what's wrong with a black woman preferring white men? Are you serious?"

We continued to debate, but in the end we were the same

women as when we began the conversation, because we still disagreed. The only change, now that I think about it, is that we disliked each other a little bit.

It's easy to think of why I liked Cecilia. She was the best friend I'd always wanted. When she let you in, she was a mother and a sister and a friend all at once. She didn't laugh or act surprised when I told her that I was still a virgin. She only nodded and said, "We have to get you laid." Around Cecilia I was more beautiful. Sometimes she would look at me and say, "You're so pretty," and coming from her it felt true. We walked around the city with coffee in our hands— with Cecilia I learned to enjoy coffee—as we explored different neighborhoods, browsing stores we couldn't afford, our conversations alternating between meaningful and carefree. It reminded me of a few years earlier, exploring the city with Malik, Baby, and José, all of us still technically kids, and how watching a bearded person strut by in green high heels on Christopher Street made me feel that life had so much possibility.

It was on one of those walks that Cecilia told me that she used to make herself throw up when she was sixteen. I told her that one of my high school teachers pushed his hand into the back of my jeans, grabbing my ass, and I had let him because I didn't know what else to do. I didn't tell anyone, but I stopped attending his class and doing any of the assignments, and when the semester ended I received an A for the class.

One of our favorite things to do was to walk along the

Hudson River. In one of the parks along the river, we discovered maybe the cleanest public bathroom in all of Manhattan. We went to places that never interested me before, like the time we went to a sex shop, and between giggles, bought vibrators. The city had never seemed more holy to me. When it got too late to go home, I'd sleep in Cecilia's dorm bed with her. She changed in front of me, stripping off her underwear as though it wasn't anything, and eventually I surprised myself by being able to do the same.

I'd never met anyone funnier than Cecilia. She was honest in the way a white girl was honest, saying the exact things in her head regardless of how personal the details of her stories were. White girls don't need to earn your trust before they talk their business. It was easy to forget that Cecilia's parents were Jamaican. Once she told me about the time her mother walked into her bedroom and caught her masturbating. Her mother was quiet for a while before she said, "I've stepped into something," and she then walked out of the room. They never talked about it. These were the kinds of stories that had us laughing too loudly when we were supposed to be studying.

I try to imagine Cecilia's life before she came to New York. Unlike the two-bedroom apartment my mother and I shared on the second floor of a house, the Wellington family residence, Cecilia told me, was an entire house with a backyard, a front yard, and an attic. Of course, they had a dog. On Saturday mornings, she and her mother would get lattes at the farmers' market, and on Mondays, when her father was off from work, he mowed the lawn. When her mother wasn't teaching economics, she was gardening, and when her father wasn't teaching chemistry, he was watching sports. It all seemed so quintessentially upper middle class.

My mother takes care of white people's children in the city—nowadays it's red-haired twins, Anna and Aaron, who are two. She never went to college, which is why it was so important that I went, and why it was so crucial that I didn't major in something as impractical as photography. Sometimes, when I was in the city, I would see black nannies pushing strollers with white children and I couldn't help thinking about my mother. It couldn't be easy spending whole days with other people's children and having to be patient with them. Once, when Cecilia and I walked past a park in the city with more than a few black nannies, she shook her head and called it—the fact that black women were caring for white babies—"modern racism." "Oh yeah, what do your parents do for a living?" I had asked. She clearly couldn't imagine the possibility that for women like my mother there weren't many options. We'd only begun hanging out and it wasn't until some time later that Cecilia learned how my mother made her money, but we never revisited that conversation.

I imagine that the Wellingtons were proud to tell people that their only daughter was studying in New York. Her parents seemed to be people who had lost some sense of who they were. When I told Cecilia that my favorite food was oxtail and that my mother was making it for my dinner, and that she should come over, she said, "Oxtail? That sounds familiar to me." She grew up eating American food. When her mother gave her cornmeal porridge, she complained and asked for boxed cereal with cold milk. Her mother wasn't like mine, who had the hard way of Caribbean mothers and therefore used to tell me that if I didn't eat what she put in front of me, then I wasn't going to eat.

Two months after Adam broke up with Cecilia, I saw him holding hands with a girl, but I didn't say anything to Cecilia because I knew it would hurt her. I'd been with Ryan, where he'd done this thing in his dorm room that involved putting his head between my legs, and when I climaxed I regretted that I wasn't invested in doing everything else with a boy who wanted to love me. Afterwards, he'd walked me out of his dormitory, where we bumped into Adam, who was holding hands with some chick. Two days later, Cecilia called me on the phone.

"Adam is fucking Lindsey," she said, crying.

"Who's Lindsey?" I asked.

"This girl I used to hang out with last year. Do you think they were fucking when he and I were together?"

"No, not necessarily. They could have hooked up afterwards."

"I know, but it's, like, so suspicious. He told me that he didn't want to be in a serious relationship and now he's in a serious relationship."

"Fuck him. You can do so much better."

"I know. But she's so skinny. When he was with me, he

told me that he doesn't like when women are too skinny and that blondes are overrated."

"What are you doing right now?" I asked, but she ignored me.

"Lindsey is one of those girls who would scheme, waiting for the opportunity to snatch a man. She would do that. She fucked one of her professors, a married man, and she didn't even feel sorry about it."

"Do you want to get together? I'd have to get some work done but we can eat and talk."

"I'll come over. You're always coming here."

"Okay, I'll tell my mother to cook."

My mother liked Cecilia because she likes all smart, good-looking black people. And then when she learned that Cecilia's parents were Jamaican, she liked her even more because Cecilia wasn't the type of Jamaican my mother called a "low-life." She wasn't loud, and she didn't have a long, bright-colored weave. She asked Cecilia what were her parents' first and last names so that she could think if she knew them, and she was visibly disappointed that she didn't recognize the names.

When I told my mother that Cecilia was coming for the weekend, she said that I had to go to the Korean store to buy a few things, and then she called me over to show me the Facebook accounts of two of her high school classmates, who'd gotten married now that gay marriage was legal in New York. They were both women. One of them was pretty and curvaceous, and had been married to a man at one point, and the other one looked like a butch lesbian. "Mi cyaan believe it," my mother said. "No one love man more than Shantel and look here! Jamaican come America and marry woman. Jesus! Di devil know who fi fool."

"What if I was gay?" I asked.

"Are you gay?" My mother turned to me, suddenly interested.

"No."

"Good."

I was sent to the Korean store to buy coconut milk for the rice and peas and a packet of curry for the chicken. I don't know for sure that the woman at the counter is Korean. Caribbean people believe that all the Asian people who own those small grocery stores that sell the spices, packaged food, and ground provisions from back home are Korean, and maybe this is true. When I exited the store, I saw that amongst the small crowd of people leaving the train station was Cecilia. A boy who looked about our age, in baggy jeans and sneakers, was talking animatedly to her, and she was smiling as though she believed him to be handsome. Meanwhile, I was wondering if Cecilia wasn't a little shocked whenever she left Manhattan for the parts of Brooklyn that weren't gentrified yet. I couldn't imagine living in a place with a Starbucks on the corner and an H&M and a bougie sandwich shop on the same block. I was surprised when I saw that Cecilia was giving the guy with the baggy jeans her number.

She told me his name was Troy. He called her an hour later.

When she hung up, she said, "He wants to be a rapper, so this is obviously not meant to be. But isn't he so hot? I swear my panties got wet just talking to him."

"Since I've known you, this is the first black guy you've been attracted to," I told her, surprised that this was a thing that was happening. "Hold on, my brain might explode from shock," I said, which made Cecilia laugh. At the very least, I could have imagined her with the type of black guy who went to Yale—certainly not a wanna-be rapper from Brooklyn. I would've been surprised if Cecilia could recite a single line from a Tupac song.

The following night, Cecilia invited Troy to come with us to a party on the Upper West Side. Zoe, a girl Cecilia knew, was having the party, and I could tell from the size of the apartment that her parents were wealthy. Cecilia, Troy, and I were the only black people there. When I walked into the living room and saw Adam and Lindsey, I immediately questioned whether Cecilia had brought Troy to make Adam jealous. It seemed like the kind of thing she'd do. She could be more fragile than I preferred in a friend—always wanting me to validate her feelings, which were many and sensitive. It seemed as though we were always having the same conversations. I imagined that as an only child, she had been coddled— her parents asking how her day was and actually listening, quick to knead every one of her anxieties away. But there was also a little of that Jamaican wildness in Cecilia. She was the woman from a movie we once watched together, that woman with mascara running down her face, the quiet one, now standing in the rain in her lingerie because she had to beg the man to stay with her. Cecilia could be dramatic like that. Once, on a bus, I heard someone say that Jamaicans are the comedians of the Caribbean. But I think it's more true that we're the performers of the Caribbean. And that night as we walked into the party, I doubted that Cecilia would wear a dress that tight and such bright red lipstick without some kind of motive.

Cecilia led Troy over to where Adam and Lindsey were sitting on the couch, and I was surprised when she bent to hug the both of them. Later, when I was waiting to use the bathroom, and it was Cecilia who exited, she whispered to me, "You should have seen how Lindsey looked at Troy. Apparently she wants to fuck every man I'm with." After that I don't know what happened, because Ryan and I sneaked off to another bathroom down the hall. Recently, Cecilia had said, "All you and Ryan do is kiss and go down on each other. You can't have an adult relationship without real sex." But it also wasn't an adult relationship because he only re-membered me when he saw me. Otherwise, he only texted once in a while. When Ryan and I were finished, and I was looking in the mirror to fix my hair, I finally said what I'd been thinking.

"How long are we going to keep doing this?" I asked. What I meant was, *When are you going to take me on a real date?*

"As long as it's fun for both of us," Ryan said, reaching to hold one of my hands.

"It's not fun for me anymore," I said, daring him to ask why.

"Okay, whatever you want," he said, and I hated that he looked as self-possessed as white men always look to me. When he left, closing the door behind him, I regretted all the times I let him eat me out and especially the times I reciprocated.

"I thought you don't date white men," Cecilia had said, when I finally told her what Ryan and I were doing.

"I didn't say I don't date white men."

"Are you sure?"

"I said I date white men but I prefer black men."

"Mmmm," she said, but I could tell that I'd lost some kind of debate I didn't even realize we'd been having.

When I got back to the living room, I was fighting the urge to cry. Troy, Lindsey, Ryan, and almost everyone else were nowhere to be seen. Later, I would learn that they were on the roof smoking the weed that Troy had brought with him. Meanwhile, Adam and Cecilia were having an intense conversation on the couch. They were talking softly, their bodies leaning toward each other, the gravity of their words on their faces.

Later, everyone was eating the Chinese food that Zoe had ordered and paid for after having rejected the offers to pitch in. One of the girls, a redhead named Kath, started talking about the latest episode of *Girls*. By this time I'd drunk too many rum and Cokes. I didn't know what else to do. Ryan had left the party with another girl, and had the audacity to hug me before he left. Cecilia whispered that the girl he left with was only his friend. But I was only a friend, which is why I couldn't help feeling jealous and more than a little crazy.

This is how come when *Girls* came up I said too loudly, "I fucking hate that show."

"Since when do you hate it? We watch it together," Cecilia said, giggling. It was true. We'd watched it together, and I was surprised that I'd found it to be charming at times. It was true that there were no black people, underrepresentation blah blah blah, but I couldn't imagine any of the characters having black friends unless the black friends were as whitewashed as they were. Cecilia would have fit right in.

"Do you hate it because it lacks racial diversity? That's the only complaint I've heard," Adam said.

"Not entirely. I really can't imagine Hannah or any of her friends having poc friends. Or at least not any poc friends who don't share the same class and ideologies as they do."

Two people laughed. I noticed that Cecilia looked uncomfortable, but I didn't care.

"So why don't you like the show then?" Kath asked.

"Because I think it glorifies gentrification. A few years back there were neighborhoods where I wouldn't see a single white person and now I see white people everywhere. White people walking their dogs. White people jogging. White people like Hannah live in neighborhoods that were overrun with minorities and immigrants but now the minorities can't afford it. White people move in, rent goes up, and coffee shops and yoga studios are opened. It's all so fucked up."

Someone, a boy I didn't know, asked, "But what are we supposed to do if we can't afford the rent in other neighborhoods?"

"I just think it's ironic the same white people who were rallying when that policeman shot that man are the same white people who move into minority neighborhoods and then the minorities are unable to afford the increased rent. White people oppress us without even trying."

Everyone, all ten of them sitting on the couches and carpeted floor, stayed silent for a moment, and then someone said, "I'm too high for this conversation." The laughter helped with the tension.

After the party had disintegrated, Cecilia and I walked to the train station. We were too buzzed to murmur anything besides how badly we yearned for a warm bed. We had planned to spend the night in Cecilia's dorm room, as it was too late to travel all the way to Brooklyn. I watched as she reached into her bag for a tube of lotion. I had no idea why, so late at night, she was rubbing lotion into her hands. She kept tubes in all of her purses. I teased her about it—that incessant need to moisturize throughout the day—but I wondered if growing up dark-skinned in a place like the Bay Area had done a number on her. "You're terrified of ashy skin, aren't you?" I once half joked.

Sometimes, I really did feel sorry for Cecilia because her upbringing meant there were so many black references that she was completely unaware of—one time I brought up the television show *Girlfriends* and was horrified to discover that she'd never heard of it. She had only ever been to Jamaica as a baby, and then for her high school senior trip, when she and her classmates had stayed at a resort. Every time her parents visited, she was in school or otherwise unable to go, and no one had thought it important enough for her to see the version of Jamaica not printed on postcards in resort gift shops. How could I describe to her the white flesh of a Jamaican apple—an apple totally unlike any American one? How could she understand my disappointment when I moved to Brooklyn as a child and discovered that the apple I loved was unavailable to me in this new place? How could she understand the loss of not being able to eat a fruit I picked by hand in my grandmother's yard? How to have a conversation about the fact that some things, some parts of ourselves, are tied to other, faraway places? These kinds of silences between Cecilia and me felt as though something had been stolen from us. Who was to blame? Her parents? White supremacy? Assimilation? And why did it matter to me that she understood and appreciated our shared heritage?

"So Adam and I are having coffee tomorrow," Cecilia said then, slathering the lotion between her fingers.

"Why?" I asked, shaking my head to refuse the tube of lotion.

"What do you mean why?"

"I literally mean why when I say 'why.' What is the point of getting coffee?"

"We're trying to be friends maybe. Tonight I asked him if he was fucking Lindsey when we were together. I told him I

was surprised they're hanging out since when we were together the both of us would always say that we kind of hated
Lindsey, and he was always saying that he didn't like women
who were too skinny. So he explained that they're, like, not a
serious thing and that he still misses and loves me but since
he's traveling abroad next semester he isn't into a long-term
relationship."

"Did you really use a black dick to make a white man jealous?"

"What are you talking about?"

"Did you only bring Troy to make Adam jealous?" Troy
had left the party earlier because he had another commitment somewhere in Brooklyn.

"Yeah, but it doesn't have anything to do with him being
black."

"So the first time you actually claim to be attracted to a
black man, it's actually because you want to make a white
man jealous? You don't see how fucked up that is?"

"Everything is about race with you."

"And not enough is about race with you."

"You embarrassed me tonight. All those things you were
saying about gentrification and *Girls*, you embarrassed me."

"I embarrassed you?"

"You came across as the eternally offended black woman."

"That's because we are eternally being disrespected."

Cecilia was shaking her head at me.

"Black people like you don't have to think about race as
much as the rest of us do."

"What are you talking about?"

"In many ways middle-class black people have the same ideologies as white people. Because more than any of us, they want what white people have. Your parents are Jamaican and you don't know anything about the country—"

"Fuck you," Cecilia said, and I could see that she meant it. In the past we would say "Fuck you" between giggles.

"You're a nigga like the rest of us," I said then, and I meant it too.

She turned and started walking away from me.

"My nigga? My nigga?" I called after Cecilia, taunting her half jokingly, and reminding her who we were, but she just kept on walking away from me. I'd wanted a reaction from her.

I'd seen ahead. I'd had some sense of the consequences but I'd said what I said anyway. In part because I meant it and in part because I wanted to hurt Cecilia for complicated reasons including the fact that she seemed to carry a lighter burden on her back. She could forget herself. She would graduate without loans because her parents could afford to pay for her tuition. She could want to sleep with a white man and that desire came as a clean feeling. I envied her for reasons that weren't even her fault. When Cecilia walked away from me, I don't know why I was surprised. I only know that I was. I stood there on West Seventy-second, waiting and hoping that she would turn around, but I was too stubborn and maybe even too stupid to make any attempts at winning back my best friend's favor. And anyway, I don't know what I would have said.

MASH UP LOVE

Mama used to say that sinful things happen before light comes back in the sky. That's how ignorant, how country, she was. She believed that when light isn't there to keep people careful, they do what they wouldn't ordinarily do. She lived by these warnings too, because I never saw her out at night, except church on Sunday and Wednesday nights, and if Cobby and I weren't with her then, she always asked Old Henry to walk her home. Every morning I wake up early enough to run while it's still dark, and sometimes I remember how Mama used to warn us about nighttime evil. One time Cobby ran home chased by three boys. One of them, a rough boy named Roger Boxx, threatened to cut my brother because he'd tried to ease his way on Roger's girl.

Cobby took off his white T-shirt and stuffed it into his briefs so that he could slip into the darkness. I was reading in the front room and Mama was sitting next to me, falling asleep and waking every other moment because she was too tired to get up and climb into bed, when Cobby knocked on the door. We looked at the bulge in front of him. Since he found his way home safely, it all seemed funny to him. He laughed as he told us about the three boys chasing him, and he made sure not to mention the girl until after Mama had gone to bed. But before Mama got up from the chair, the tiredness seemed to have faded from her, and she shook her head at Cobby. "Dats why mi warn yuh 'bout walk di street ah night," she said. "But yuh don't want fi listen to nothing mi sey." Then she closed her bedroom door. Back then, Cobby and I looked forward to the time of night when Mama retired to her room. The front room, where we slept and ate and did our living, became a playground, a confessional, and a reprieve in that two-room house after she went to bed.

I cut one of the limes Ann-Marie picks from the tree behind our house and I squeeze half of it into a cup, adding brown sugar and cold water from the fridge. Only a little sweet drink can wake me up and keep my body light enough to run. A long time ago, I watched a race on the television where a black man much blacker than me beat a whole bunch of white people and he smiled into the camera and his teeth were like sunlight forcing my eyes closed. That's how bright his teeth shone with skin that black. He pointed up to God, maybe to say, "You was the one who made these legs to work so fast." I started running after that. Don't know why, it just

felt like something a powerful type of man should do. This
was back when I had just come from the country to attend
university. I didn't know anybody and didn't know how to
know anybody—the world closes up for a quiet man. I
started running when it was dark because I was ashamed for
anyone to see my stick legs doing anything beyond walking.
Ann-Marie says I'm greedy for such a small man. What she
doesn't understand is that I'm eating more than enough so
that I don't become an even smaller man because of all the
running I do.

I touch my toes and then I stretch each leg on one of the
low branches of the mango tree in our front yard. I start out
slow, feeling the last of my sleep slip off, and eventually my
legs feel stronger and then I am gaining speed. I always loop
around our housing scheme, admiring the gleam of new
houses built on what used to be bush. A few of the houses
are still empty. They all tend to be larger than ours, with
more expansive lawns. We wanted something more modest
with trees mature enough to produce fruit—the only house
in the scheme that hadn't been built brand-new. I wanted to
live in a house where Mama could visit and feel comfortable.
She liked nice things but she was born and would die a countrywoman, so she was easily overwhelmed. When she lived
with us, she looked around at the neighbors' houses and
asked, "So a wah? People wid money want dem 'ouse fi come
white?" In the country, we never knew a white house. People
who didn't have the money left their houses the color of the
cement blocks, while others painted their walls the color of
dirt or leaves or the sky, anything but white.

If people who know me could hear all the talk going on in my head while I run, they would be surprised. Because not only am I quiet, but I am also simple. Everything about me is quiet and simple—from the clothes I put on, to the ordinary way I talk that doesn't bring attention for being an educated man, to the unfussy way I gratefully eat everything that Ann-Marie puts in front of me. It's a combination that continues to surprise people when they hear how well I've done for myself. When they see the woman I'm with, they take a good look at her light skin and tall hair and they wonder how a Mawga foot man could get a woman like that. They don't realize I can see the surprise in their faces as they look from Ann-Marie to me. They wouldn't guess that my demeanor is what caught Ann-Marie's eyes at UWI. Her father, a louder, bigger man, used to beat her mother, so I believe she took my quiet ways to mean I would treat her good, and I have. I knew cockier, more talkative men were looking her way, and because I didn't think she would consider me, I didn't think anything when she created opportunities to talk to me. One day she asked if I wanted a piece of the coconut drops she was eating in the last moments before our Human Resources class began. I looked past her to Devon Taylor, the handsomest boy in our class, whose people had money because his father was somehow involved in Parliament. Devon Taylor was looking at Ann-Marie, she was looking at me, and in that moment I considered how often she offered food to me and the times she bumped into me studying at my usual spot in the library. It didn't make sense, but I put two and two together. It bothered me that my nature—which had caused

people to misuse and ignore me all my life, especially in comparison to Cobby's—could catch a woman's attention because of the safety of being loved by a man like me. I started
meeting Ann-Marie's interest with my own.

The next time Ann-Marie showed up at my study spot in
the library, I told her I'd heard about a girl who was selling
fried fish from her dorm room and I asked if she wanted to
come with me to buy some. Every time that girl, I think her
name was Keisha, went home, she came back to campus with
a whole bunch of fried fish her mother and little sisters
helped her fry, since her people lived by the sea and her father fished for a living. Keisha worked in the cafeteria at
UWI, and selling fried fish was a way for her to make a little
extra money. She always came back to campus late on Sunday nights, and by the following night all the fish would be
sold. When sales were especially busy, customers had to
form a line inside her dorm room.

If I could pinpoint the exact moment when Ann-Marie
and I started to come together, I would say it began with sitting on Keisha's bed in a room crowded with customers,
watching her lift two fried fish out of a pan. Keisha didn't
even ask if we wanted the fish wrapped separately. I saw how
she looked from Ann-Marie's face to mine, wondering how a
country boy like me had anything to do with a pastor's
daughter. Those of us at UWI who came from nothing, we
always could tell each other apart. Keisha could tell from the
cleanliness of the few tired clothes I owned. If we had taken
a class together, she might have been able to tell from how
hard I worked, as though working was going out of style. She

could imagine that I was raised on whatever edible our yard and the yards of our neighbors bore and the little meat my mother could acquire every now and then. Still, sitting on that bed, it occurred to me that Ann-Marie was mine; maybe I even guessed that I would marry her. It all felt powerful to me. Keisha and I came from the same type of place and I knew that Ann-Marie and I were going to eat what seemed to me to carry a little of the hope of country people. Though it could be that I alone rested meaning on those moments in Keisha's bedroom and none of it ever occurred to Ann-Marie.

Just as I'm running past the biggest house in the scheme, where a white man and a woman Ann-Marie said tried out for Miss Jamaica live, Cobby comes on my mind. Just as how Ann-Marie says God whispers in her ear sometimes, warning that she's going to buck up on the exact person she doesn't want to buck up on. It's with that kind of certainty that I know I will see Cobby today, even though I haven't seen him from before Mama's funeral, and he is not the kind of man you can easily catch to beg back for the money he begged off you for a long time now.

There are pregnant women who say that they can feel the bodies pushing against each other, already in competition, as if to speak to whatever it is that erupts when one seed is no longer one, when one seed becomes two. As soon as I could piece any understanding together, I started reading and re-reading the parts of the Bible where my name comes up. Because Rebekah felt Esau and Jacob fighting inside her, I always imagined Mama felt my brother and me, especially as we got older and started to turn in opposite directions. In my mind, if God spoke as clearly to Mama as He did to Rebekah, He would speak of the prophecy of two brothers not even opening their mouths to taste the air outside the womb and already struggling to stand taller than each other. *Two nations are in thy womb, and two manner of people shall be separated from thy bowels; and the one shall be stronger than the other people; and the older shall serve the younger.* When I first read this, young as I was and only half understanding, a part of me knew it was too late, that Cobby had already beat me.

I don't think Mama, a true countrywoman, read ten books in her life. Even the Bible that sat on the dresser by her bed, and which Mama cautioned my brother and me never to put any other book on top of, I rarely saw her open. This would have been a surprise for anyone who knew Mama well, who saw that she was often the first one to get up when the pastor made an altar call or asked for a testimony. Yes, I grew up hearing Mama give testimonies in church, stringing the Bible verses she knew together to make points about salvation or waiting on the Lord, then ending the testimony with a hymn. She spoke too long and she couldn't sing, the whole congregation seemed to sigh and my brother and I held our heads in shame whenever Mama made it to the front of the church, and she never missed an opportunity to testify.

When we were growing up, Mama often complained that reading the Bible made her eyes hurt, so she would close her eyes for a little to relax them and then she would fall asleep. Sometimes Mama, my brother, and I would be walking down the road and Mama would ask, "A who dat a cum up di road? A Hyacinth dat?" Mama's eyes bothered her. She needed glasses. I don't know that Mama would have named us Jacob and Esau if the story was one that she read for herself. Sibling jealousy, parental favoritism, and familial deceit—I don't know that Mama would have given us this legacy if she knew better. I imagine she heard the names of the biblical twins from various religious leaders her entire life attending church. Because she wanted to give us biblical names, when she pushed us out and saw that we were two, and male, Mama named my brother Jacob—Cobby—and she named me Esau.

Mama said her whole life, as far back as she could remember, she was trying to see. She was always squinting her eyes and walking close to food or animals or people and using her hands to tell her what her eyes couldn't. Which is why my long-dead grandmother often chastised Mama when she was a girl, "Yuh always have fi touch everyt'ing." Mama's favorite food was fried dumplings. She could always smell my grandmother frying the dumplings, but not until Mama could poke the cooling dumplings would she be satisfied. As a little girl, she thought everyone's eyes saw the world as fuzzy as she did. This is why it never occurred to her to complain to her teacher or parents. The day Mama realized something was wrong, the teacher wrote a word she couldn't see and then the teacher called on her to pronounce it. Mama guessed "cat" because it was one of the words that often came up in the teacher's spelling lessons. The teacher might have looked

at Mama funny, Mama didn't say, but she heard the class
laughing at her. Someone else was called to read the word
and it was "mango."

Only in Mama's later years did she get a good pair of
glasses. Twice in the past someone had brought her reading
glasses packed safely in a barrel from the States. The first pair
Mama received because my grandmother begged a favor of a
neighbor whose people were sending her a barrel. This pair
Mama kept until two or so years after my brother and I were
born—she always said she thanked God for letting her see us
so clearly after she pushed us out. But one day, Mama left the
glasses within reach of my baby brother, who broke them.
For a long time after, Mama still wore the glasses, she just
had them taped together, until the tape loosened hold and
one of the lenses fell under her foot while she was walking.
After that, Mama kept the other lens in her brassiere for safe-
keeping. She would hold the lens to the Bible when the pastor said to turn to a verse or when she wanted to look at the
chicken back she was buying from the meat man. Mama got
a second pair when I was ten years or so. She asked someone
going to foreign to bring her back a pair of glasses. But the
second pair was too strong, it pained Mama's eyes, so she
laid it on her dresser next to her Bible and continued keeping
the lens in her brassiere.

Not until I attended UWI, and I brought her into the city
to see where I was living and going to school, did Mama go
to an eye doctor, who checked her eyes and prescribed glasses
that catered to her vision needs. "A neva see so good inna mi
life," Mama said. When she put the glasses on for the first

time, her whole face was smiling. "Dis is how God mek mi eyes before sin clog it up." Later when I visited her, I saw that she kept the new pair of glasses next to her Bible, and when I pointed this out and asked her why she wasn't wearing the glasses, she said, "A mi Bible glasses dat." At the time, I was annoyed that she allowed me to use the money I could have used for textbooks to buy a pair of glasses that she wasn't wearing. When I knocked on the door holding the little plastic bag containing a package of tripe, I expected Mama to answer the door with the glasses on her face. That day I sat in my annoyance, and finally it lifted and hovered over me and mixed with the smell of the onions, garlic, and tripe. I watched as Mama took the lens from her brassiere to check the tripe. Then she was lifting the boiling pot cover and using the lens to check on the dumplings and green bananas.

Mama is buried five months now and Cobby didn't come to the funeral. I have no doubt he received the news. I don't know why he didn't come, but I wasn't surprised because this is the kind of man my brother is. I even asked Lennox, my wife's brother, to be a pallbearer in case Cobby didn't show up. Days before the funeral, I drove to the houses of the various women my brother has children with, since apparently he sometimes keeps the mothers as lovers. I imagine this quiets their concerns about his inability to financially care for his children. But none of the women had seen Cobby recently. One of them suggested he might be in jail again for reckless behavior while overdrinking. All of them com-

plained about him; one of them started to cry. I opened my
wallet and not one of them refused the money.

I'm watching Ann-Marie drop the dumplings in the oil,
gently so as not to make the oil jump up on her. I've been
sitting here at the table for twenty minutes now, since I
walked into the house and sat down still wearing my suit.
Ann-Marie can tell that something is paining me, but she is
allowing me to dwell in it as long as I need to. That's how I
know I married the right woman. Ann-Marie respects my
need for silence. Before I met her, I had only been with one
other woman, Roxanne, who had to fill every silence, wanting to know, "Why yuh face look so?"

Soon I'll tell Ann-Marie what's bothering me. But right
now it stretches over me, and I want to hold it in my hands a
little longer. Just like how God whispered, I saw Cobby today.
I went for lunch with my secretary, Scarlet, a big-boned
woman who I love like a sister. She loves food like no woman
I've ever known, which is why Ann-Marie and I laugh at her
and call her Love Food Scarlet behind her back. We were in
the market looking to buy jerk chicken from one of the men
who roast meat in steel drums when Scarlet said, "But dat
man fava you?" I looked over, immediately worried she
meant Cobby. There he was, hungrily eating a mango and
talking, gesturing as if what he was saying was important. He
is the kind of man who displays importance while talking
foolishness. The man he was talking with appeared to be the
bus driver. My brother has never had grand ambitions for
himself. For a living he takes a small cut from the bus driver
for the customers he rallies together so that they get on his

driver's bus instead of someone else's. No wonder he can't support his children. From the way he was opening his mouth to laugh, I could see the two missing teeth on his left side. He was laughing, his whole body bent over, laughing like a man who doesn't have one fret in the world. Maybe he doesn't. Maybe his children aren't his concerns when he puts his head down at night. I always thought of him as having less shame than I have. I fixed my teeth as soon as I left the country and got my first job. "That's my brother," I said to Scarlet. She must have heard in my voice that I didn't feel like saying anything else, and then I was walking away, even as she stood there watching my brother. We bought the chicken and walked back to the office. Neither of us brought up Cobby.

The last time I saw him, he was in the middle of chasing a woman. It was during the busiest time of Mandeville Square, when the day is ending and people are heading home from their various commitments. I had just come out of the supermarket because Ann-Marie called me that afternoon and asked me to bring home a few packets of banana chips and cream sodas. She had been sick with the flu and heavy food wouldn't stay in her stomach. When I exited the supermarket, I saw Cobby talking to two other men in front. A young woman passed by, Cobby grabbed after her hand and held on to her fingers, and the woman pulled her fingers free.

But when she turned to face my brother, anyone could see that he flattered her. From where I was standing, I couldn't see Cobby's face, but I could see the young woman's face shining under the sweet words of my brother. He always knew what to tell women, even Mama. "Mama, mek mi help yuh carry dat bag." "Mama, mi like when yuh do yuh hair so." "Mama, mi was telling mi friend dat none of dem mother look as good as my old lady." He knew the right combination of words to open them up, so that even though they could see that he was a womanizer, they could forget for a sweet little while until the belly came along and my brother grew scarce and the women wanted to kick themselves for getting involved with him in the first place.

Mama used to talk about a "mash up" kind of love. This kind of love would often lead to some kind of slackness involving a married man or a pregnant schoolgirl or a woman dealing with a man everyone told her not to deal with. Mama used this term around her churchwomen friends when they discussed various people who were led from the road to Calvary because they couldn't quiet the way their hearts would pinch them.

The one time I experienced mash up love was with a girl named Jordan, who lived with her grandma down the road. When I discovered her in church one day, when I saw the little red bows on the shoes sticking out from the legs further down in the pew, my head traveled up from the prettiest pair of shoes I ever saw to the sweetest face I ever saw. She had just moved from America, since her parents thought it would be valuable if their fourteen-year-old left the jungles of Brooklyn to be educated in the Jamaican way by her grandmother. The girls in the church simultaneously admired and despised her. When they weren't complimenting her clothes and accent, they were talking about how she thought she was better than them, which seemed to be completely unfounded since they couldn't provide any examples but just agreed with each other that Jordan was "bad mind." I stood next to them behind the pit toilet at the back of the church, pretending I wasn't listening but was waiting until they finished talking so I could tell one of them that her mother sent me to call her.

It wasn't long before I used every opportunity to walk past Jordan's grandmother's house or to cut through their yard. Sometimes I wasted my time because the yard was bare, but other times I saw Jordan washing her and her grandmother's clothes in the yard. I always waved to her and she waved back, and sometimes we exchanged pleasantries when she initiated it. The whole thing fueled and devastated me because we never moved toward any kind of familiarity.

Instead, Jordan told the other girls from church that I was following her around in school and church, and even showing up in her yard. When the news came back to me, I stopped walking through her yard, and when I walked past her house I looked straight ahead. Later, I couldn't be upset with Cobby when he and Jordan's name started running together, because I had never told him I loved her. By this time, we were moving toward manhood, Cobby sprinting faster toward it. Although he and I weren't close like we were as boys, I knew he respected me. Just like how he wouldn't have allowed the boys in our district to laugh at me because I enjoyed reading, wasn't any good at cricket, and was never linked to any kind of intimacy with a girl, he wouldn't have become involved with Jordan if he knew I wanted her.

Jordan was the girl Cobby got pregnant when he was sixteen, a little more than a year after she'd left her home in Brooklyn. They said that although her period refused to greet her for two months, Ms. Honey only put two and two together a week before Jordan was supposed to return to Brooklyn. Ms. Honey had taught Jordan how to wash clothes with her hands, whispering to Mama that at first her granddaughter couldn't even wash her panties without a machine and shaking her head because it was troubling to her how foreign caused people to pack up their dirty drawers, allowing them to sit before they could stuff them into a machine with the rest of their clothes. Ms. Honey was thinking she did a good job squeezing the slack American ways out of her granddaughter when it hit her that she hadn't seen any evidence of her granddaughter's period in two months. In the barrels her daughter sent from foreign, packages of maxi pads were included, and Ms. Honey had shown Jordan how to wrap the used maxi pad in old pieces of newspaper. But Ms. Honey hadn't seen Jordan go into the drawer for newspaper in weeks.

Jordan never looked in my brother's direction nor he in hers, they were never seen together, but everybody knew. Here was a fifteen-year-old with hardly any breasts in front of her carrying my brother's child. Mama was probably the last to know. Because she presented herself as such a pious figure in the community, no one knew how to tell her. But eventually it reached Mama's ears, and she threw the bucket of dirty water she used to clean the floors on Cobby. He walked out of the yard, his clothes dripping, and he didn't come back until three days later. By then, Mama didn't seem as angry anymore, although for a long time she carried a burden in her face, which seemed to me to encompass the gravity of the whole thing but especially the shame my brother had brought on her shoulders, revealing her family as spiritually flawed.

My brother was seventeen when Jordan had the baby. It squeezed out of her without any life in it. But this was all talk, since none of us saw the baby. One week Jordan was pregnant in church, and two weeks later she was back in Brooklyn. No one said it but I could see the relief in the faces of Mama, Cobby, and Ms. Honey. Soon after, Mama testified in church. I don't remember what she said, but I remember that Cobby, who has started coming to church again, was listening because I saw that their eyes were making four, they were talking to each other. Cobby didn't get another woman pregnant till he was twenty.

We were so different from early on. Mama said I was a quiet baby, while Cobby cried if she wasn't looking at him. Mama used to tell people a funny story about how she used to put a big teddy bear on the dresser so that Cobby would think someone was in the room with him. It worked for a while and then he wanted more than someone's presence, he wanted Mama's hands on him. This was her way of telling how he always loved people from the beginning. I was the opposite. Mama used to describe my personality as "funny." I was afraid of anyone I didn't know, and even the ones I did know. Cobby would walk forward to meet people but I always stayed behind with Mama.

Then in grade school Cobby couldn't keep his behind in the seat for five minutes. He wasn't a bad child, everyone liked him, classmates and teachers alike, he just lived a careless life—always forgetting to do his homework, to study for exams, to bring his lunch from home—and it might have seemed worse when compared to the neatness of my life. Later, when I scored the highest on the common entrance exam, the church helped to send me to college.

Still, everyone preferred my brother. People respected me but they preferred him. Here was Cobby, with his big laugh, and the way his eyes took in everybody, making even old churchwomen nobody paid any mind feel seen. Here was Cobby, cracking jokes and memorizing the names of even the least of people. He had friends all over. Here was Cobby with the same face as me, yet the way his face and his body filled out, maybe because he always had a big appetite, he was better to look at. People would look past me to rest their eyes on the other twin. They could barely tell us apart, and yet somehow Cobby begged to be looked at.

We would come home from grade school, my uniform would still be clean and Cobby's would be stained with the red dirt from behind our school. Mama would shake her head at Cobby—that was all. All my life I waited for Mama to have a stronger reaction to the many ways my brother shamed himself and our family. But she always just shook her head, her expression becoming more pained with the severity of my brother's actions. I imagined us as accomplices,

Mama and I, shaking our heads together. I wanted to hear about the ways I had grown into a superior man, because if I did it for anyone, I did it for her. But if I listened for anything, I listened for silence.

Three months before Mama died, she came to live with us. She kept asking for Cobby. None of us had seen him in months. I usually bumped into him around Mandeville Square, and every time, his whole face smiled, and he would tell anyone around him that I was the one who took all the ambition. We always talked as friends who meant to keep in contact but never got around to it. Every once in a while, he would make it to Mama's house with a plastic bag containing tripe. As bad as her eyes were, she never made the mistake of mixing us up when we were growing up. But in her last months, Mama's memory was deteriorating. She sometimes called me Cobby, and at times she would ask, "Why yuh nah be'ave yuhself?" But she would say it softly, as if she didn't really care for an answer, as if she might as well have been whispering how much she loved him.

A steep road was the only way for cars to get to our house. And only people with dusty cars, already busted-up cars, would brave the potholes in our road. Nobody vain about his car ever drove by our house. For years, I looked forward to the day when I would walk down to the bottom of the hill and escape the sun for a long time under the soursop tree to wait for a taxi going into the city. In one hand would be the worn suitcase Mama kept under her bed with other things

she never had use for, and in my other hand a briefcase because it seemed to me that men who did important things
carried briefcases. Now I realize that my ambition wasn't as
much for me as it was for everyone else. Leaving Mama, my
brother, our district, was to be the loudness everybody desired from me. In my mind, the man under the soursop tree
looked and seemed older, as if it was indeed time to leave
home and his face looked comforted in the realization. But
the truth of it is that the man was really a boy of seventeen,
and only standing under the tree did it occur to him that he
was feeling to cry.

Now Ann-Marie is cooking up some saltfish. I can't see
what she's doing from the dining table since her back is
turned, but I hear when the chopped onion, scallion, and
tomato hit the hot oil in the frying pan. After nine years of
marriage I've memorized the ways Ann-Marie seasons food.
I don't have to watch her to know she will start the saltfish
with three promises: onion, scallion, and tomato. The smell
carries to my nose, and for the first time since I walked into
the house and sat down, my body longs for the present, longs
to be fed. Ann-Marie always cooks the saltfish at the tail end
since it comes together quickly, so I know I won't have to
wait long to eat and this realization comforts me. I can see
her body over the pan and I imagine that she is stirring the
tomato, onions, and scallions that are softening over the fire,
releasing the flavor and the juice that the saltfish will be
cooked in. Then I see her moving over the sink and I know
she is throwing the water off the fish. I close my eyes and
push my head against the back of the chair. I smell that the

flavor in the air has changed. She has added the fish to the pan. Next she will add pepper.

Nine years. Ann-Marie and I have been married for nine years already. It doesn't even feel half that long. We keep trying but she has still been unable to get pregnant. Sometimes I look at the life I have built—I got the job and the woman I wanted—and it is not enough. Because the woman I wanted to see me for everything I've done, all of it so that she could look at me with pride in her heart, never loved me for the ways I was better than my brother. And then there is the other thing that cuts deeper, that I don't want to think about when I can help it, and which I have kept buried so deep I've never slipped and confessed it to Ann-Marie. It's that she and I will never produce children, while I can't keep track of the number of children Cobby has fathered.

"I saw Cobby today," I finally confess out loud.

"Yeah? What was he saying?" Ann-Marie doesn't turn from cooking.

"You know, we didn't get a chance to talk."

She looks at me now. "Oh, dat brother of yours. Lawd Jesus, how 'im cum so?"

This was a conversation Ann-Marie and I have had many times in the past. Nothing was ever resolved. We asked the same questions and came to the same conclusions, that my brother mystified us both.

"A true yuh mother spoil him."

I think about it. I have always thought about it. Had Mama spoiled him? She loved him, even for the ways he fell short, which I could never do. If she gave one of us a suck-

suck, she gave one to the other. When she beat me for taking a slice of the fruit cake she made for the pastor, she also beat Cobby for taking a slice. Did she spoil him? She never compared Cobby to me like our teachers did. She always accepted him as her prodigal son, the one who went off and shamed her, but when he came back, she rejoiced. I stood in the background wondering about my prize for never leaving in the first place. Did she spoil him? I can't say, so I don't answer, allowing Ann-Marie's assessment to fall between us.

"Yuh tink 'bout dat ting yet?" Ann-Marie asks now, her back intentionally turned to me.

Her company wants to transfer her to the United States. Last week when Ann-Marie received the offer, she arranged for us to meet at our favorite restaurant for dinner. I laughed at her because she was behaving like it was the weekend, ordering a whole fried fish for each of us, and a fruity alcoholic drink for herself. When she told me about the promotion, she reminded me that in my younger years I'd wanted a PhD, and she suggested that perhaps we could look into fertility treatment and adopting children. She seemed certain that the United States would open up our lives. I envied her certainty. A long time ago, I saw a news story about an adopted child who grew into the man that murdered both his parents, and I no longer had the desire to return to school. I had also observed that friends and family who emigrated to the United States and Canada returned for visits seeming intent on impressing those of us who stayed behind. They told stories about the wonders of abroad, their successes and the successes of their children, and the forcefulness of their telling made me suspect that perhaps foreign wasn't as heavenly as they wanted us to believe. I didn't tell Ann-Marie about any of this because I knew that if I spoke too harshly against going, she would be bitter for a long time. And perhaps in the United States, she offered while we lay in bed after we returned from the restaurant, I could forget the business with my family. "Wah business wid my family?" I had asked. "The whole thing wid yuh bredda and yuh madda and how yuh fret ova dem," she said. I was amazed that she could compact my life into so few words. Could I really forget? I wondered. Could the distance of land and sea really do that? How to live a life without the expectation that on a Tuesday afternoon I might bump into Cobby?

"Yuh tink 'bout dat ting yet?" Ann-Marie repeats, now facing me.

"What ting?" I joke, and she cuts her eyes at me.

If Mama was alive, I would never consider leaving. And now that she is gone, why not leave because I can? Perhaps Ann-Marie is right—that I no longer have to be labored by the roles of son and brother. Perhaps leaving is indeed my chance. Later, in bed, I will tell her my decision, as we tend to have our most important conversations in the dark.

Ann-Marie can see everything in my face when she puts the plates on the table. "Esau, no worry wid him," she says, rubbing the top of my head. "Cobby is him own man."

SLACK

When this story ended—or when it began, because who on June Plum Road could tell the difference?—the mermaids were floating at the top of Old Henry's tank. The green hair of one and the pink hair of the other fanned out on the water's surface, silky straight hair, and the sparkles in their tails caught the afternoon light. Old Henry laughed when he saw the dolls in his tank, a laugh he would later regret. Because when he looked beyond the mermaids, his eyes made out two forms, the little girls, beneath the water's surface.

And the mother would go mad when she heard, at least for a while, sitting on the steps in front of her house, legs wide, without panties. A shame a man passing by was the one to call out to let her know about her nakedness. Her people would send for her, and news would travel back that she is cleaning for white people in New York. Many on June Plum Road won't know what to do with this information but to wonder if she remembers to wear panties now.

Some people would say that they sensed tragedy before Old Henry found the mermaids and the girls in his tank. Lazarus said his chickens wouldn't lay eggs. After the girls were found, he walked up and down June Plum Road telling any ear he came across that when a whole dozen chickens won't lay a single egg a sensible man should start to shiver. Mrs. Thomas, who everybody called Bad Mind Thomas behind her back, dropped the malice she held toward everyone in the district to say again and again, "Oh, a dat mek di dog dem a bark so!" While she walked her dogs, she heard people talking about the drownings in front of the shop. The dogs were two fluffy yellow animals her husband brought home when her menstrual blood continued to greet her after a decade of marriage. The dogs laid up on the Thomases' couch and bed and ate out of her hands like white people on television. This is why people on June Plum Road looked at Mrs. Thomas sideways, which in turn caused her to carry malice against everybody in the district.

Miss Marie, who taught fourth grade at the primary school before she retired, said from the hungry way she saw those two little girls move toward any little bit of water with the mermaid dolls, something told her—maybe the Lord, she would add to later versions of the story—that that kind of hunger in anyone, especially children who can't think level-headed, wouldn't do anybody any good. Then there was Toni, Tall Legs Toni, who said that because her C-section scar was itching her, she knew that the Lord was trying to tell her something but what it was she didn't know. "Di Lawd works in mysterious ways," she would say to any of the women who paid to have her hot comb dragged through their hair for the Christmas church service. But nobody paid Toni's sanctimonious talk any mind. The women just fingered their newly straightened hair and kissed their teeth when they left Toni's house, because she was known to visit the Obeah man every once in a while when her man didn't come home.

The Seventh-day Adventist pastor explained to his congregation that days leading up to the drownings he started to worry that something bad was going to happen. The uneasiness even kept him up at night—some nights he would wake up with a piece of worry he had never been handed in his life. And it would be a long time before he could fall asleep again, sometimes not until the sun began to rise. He even started to believe what his mother used to say about curry—that if you ate too much and too often it made you fret. Since it was his wife's biggest pregnancy craving, he was eating curry more often than before, some days even back to back, and his wife put curry in foods he didn't think could be curried, like the scrambled eggs she put in front of him one morning. But then news came about the little girls and that night he could sleep. And because he was a crying kind of pastor, the kind whose voice would start to crack whenever he preached his Easter or Christmas sermon or presided over a funeral, he cried after telling his congregation how it turned out not to be the curry after all.

Because Old Henry drank his wife's cornmeal porridge for his midday meal and it sat heavy in his stomach and because he'd become an old man prone to paralyzing bouts of fatigue, he slept after lunch. This, even though in his younger days he used to cry shame after a man who let a meal put him back in bed. Later he would say it was as if something shook him awake. He got out of bed, and as he was going outside, his wife looked up from the peas she was shelling to ask where he was going. But he didn't pay her any mind because all he knew was that he had to go look about his tank. He thought it was the young boys yet again turning his tank into a swimming pool. As wide as the king-size mattress he and his wife slept on, and tall enough so that Old Henry's feet could almost touch the bottom, the tank was a cement structure behind the house used for collecting rainwater to wash clothes, to bathe, to boil for drinking.

His wife would tell everyone who would listen to her that a crying old man is the ugliest thing to see. "Yuh tink yuh see ugly?" she would ask. "A ole man yuh wan' fi see a cry."

Who knew what was story and what was God's truth, but only Marie opened her window the day it happened, only Marie who could have stopped it, Marie who kept silent amidst all the talk of the little girls. She saw the girls pulling a cement block in the direction of Old Henry's tank, but just before she opened her door to call out to them, she paused to turn down the fire under the pot of chicken foot soup she was cooking. And when she went back to open the door, she could only pause with her hand on the handle because she couldn't remember why she meant to open the door. Only when she heard the mother screaming—people ways over say they heard the mother screaming—did she remember. But if the screams told her anything, they told her it was too late.

But if we were to go back before it happened, Christmastime was what was on everybody's minds. Not the two little dark-skinned girls, six years old, who everyone always mixed up because they looked exactly alike and their names, Kadi-ann and Jadi-ann, were so similar. Three days after they were dead, it was Christmas Day. On June Plum Road, those who could afford to were eating the goat their husbands slaughtered, those who couldn't afford a goat were eating chicken, and those who didn't have anything made sure to be invited to the homes of those who had extra meat. But the meat took on a disappointing taste that year. Some people thought it was because they had been looking forward to Christmas dinner for so long it was bound to be disappointing. Some of the women said they anticipated it, as food never tasted good when the same hand picking the feathers off the chicken or skinning the goat and chopping up the meat, was the same hand dealing with the blood, was the same hand dealing with seasoning the meat, preparing it, and finally serving it onto plates. No one thought to blame the two little girls whose drownings dominated the Christmas dinner conversation.

. . .

The girls belonged to the slack woman, who moved to the district to live with her grandmother when her own pious mother refused to keep a pregnant teenager under her roof. The woman eventually took over her grandmother's house when the old woman died. She mothered the girls without a man and took in sewing because it was all she could do beautifully. She was a dark-skinned, dry-headed girl and not even the kind of dark skin that shone so everybody, even those who lightened their skin, had to admit that shade of brown was something to look at. Her mother used to suck on Scotch bonnet peppers when she was pregnant and then when the child came out from between her mother's legs and everybody saw she took her father's dark coloring, the name Pepper stuck. But they used to call her Blackie or Dry Head when she was in school, and no one had to tell her she wasn't the kind of woman anybody looked at more than once. Maybe that's why she lay down for the first man who paid her any mind, even though he was a married man with four children and had only three good teeth in his mouth.

When the wife heard that her husband got some young girl pregnant, she turned up at Pepper's house with a machete in her hand. Not because she was expecting to cut Pepper, since the machete was too dull, but because she wanted to look tough. No one answered the door, so she walked around to the back of the house and saw a young girl still wearing her school uniform sitting on a rock and bending over to scale fish. No one had to tell her it was her husband's baby mother. She knew because the girl looked like the right kind of weak-minded to lie down for a man with only three good teeth in his mouth.

The wife only had one question, "How ole yuh be, gyal?"

"Fifteen, ma'am."

The wife left it at that, but later she would tell someone, "Mi see di gyal mi wutless husband a run roun' wid. A one dry-head pickney who look like she could a still suck titty. Mi could a jus' look pon har an feel sorry fi di likkle fool."

When she got home, she swung the machete at her husband, but he was quick to jump out of the way.

Before the little girls drowned, all anybody knew about Pepper with any kind of conviction was that she was slack to have children for a married man. They said that even God thought to punish her, giving her two children instead of one. But she could sew beautifully. She sewed the white suits for the deaconesses at the Methodist church. When the reverend's wife, who everyone thought acted better looking than she was, saw the suits, even she had to humble herself to whisper and ask someone who sewed them.

Pepper couldn't tell she had two babies inside her—when they pressed against her belly, she felt it as one touch. She craved raw rice. She used to stand over the canister her grandmother kept the rice in, willing herself to resist the temptation, and sometimes she could. Other times she would scoop a handful into her mouth, but only when the craving felt like it would kill her. That's why when Pepper's grandmother pulled the first baby out of her granddaughter, everything looked all right until her attentive eyes made their way to the baby's back. She studied the baby's back for a few moments, finally arriving at a destination. Raw rice stuck to the baby's skin! And for a moment Pepper's grandmother held the baby in her hands because the rice did look permanent, like a disease or a disfigurement, but when she rubbed her hand across the baby's back, her hand came back bloodstained, brushing some of the rice onto the bedroom floor.

All her life, as far back as memory took her, Pepper was always craving something. First: sugar from the tin her mother kept it in. These were the days her mother used to comb Pepper's hair in two, like cow horns sticking out the sides of her head, ribbons hanging from the ends of the plaits. Pepper would scoop a little sugar between her fingers, small enough so that her mother wouldn't notice. But the cumulative occurrences always revealed the thief—plus the fact that she often forgot to reattach the lid of the canister, which invited ants into the sugar. When Pepper was a little older, she used to take a piece of dough from the large lump her mother left sitting to be made into dumplings. She would knead the dough between her dirty fingers and then push it around her mouth before finally swallowing it. Later on, when Pepper no longer wore ribbons in her hair, her mother developed a nighttime craving for water crackers dipped in tea, and Pepper eventually came to share the craving. After her mother boiled water over a smashed piece of ginger, after she poured the water into a cup and added a little sugar and a few crackers to the tea, she would start to eat the whole thing with a spoon, and Pepper would turn up next to her with a spoon of her own. Pepper didn't need to say anything. Her mother would always push the cup in her direction but not before complaining, "Yuh no feel good if yuh nah lean up pon me."

And then Pepper craved Lester. But not at first. When she first saw him at the front of the shop, playing dominoes with the other men, men her mother called "dutty" because they were idle, playing dominoes in the middle of the day, she barely noticed him. And then he threw a fresh grin her way, not because he found her attractive, but because she was there, and he was the type of Caribbean man for whom schoolgirls in their uniforms are to be admired and pursued without shame. Pepper called him "dutty" in her mind, and walked off kissing her teeth. But this was one of those things, the kind where the fruits of flattery wedge themselves where common sense, repulsion, and the fear of being seen together in public would be. This was one of those things where a more seasoned man is persistent enough, sweet-talking enough, to confuse a young girl so that she could look at his face and wonder if he couldn't do something about his teeth, maybe at least not grin so wide, while at the same time glowing under the light of his compliments. This was one of those old-time grown-man/young-girl stories, nothing unusual in its pages.

And then after he got what he wanted, Pepper lost interest. The proximity of Lester's mouth when she laid down under him, remembering everything her mother told her about how easy it was to come home with a belly, the awkwardness and rawness of the intimacy, all of it shamed her. She stayed away from the shop after that. No more passing by to see if Lester was playing dominoes. One time when Pepper was leaving the schoolyard with her friends, he was standing by the school gate waiting for her, but she pretended not to see him. One of her friends said, "Pepper, one ole man a look pon you! Mek yuh no go talk wid him?" They all laughed.

It went on like this for a while, Pepper trying to dodge the three-teeth man, all the while wondering how she could have lost her mind to lay down for such a nasty man. Eventually, Lester lost interest too. He wasn't the kind of man to chase a woman. One time, Pepper's mother gave her a basin of rice to pick and rinse. She found herself picking out and eating pearls of rice, something she had never done before. But it didn't appear out of the ordinary for her, and she wouldn't put two and two together until her period refused to greet her.

But all of that is history. When the people of June Plum Road knew her, Pepper craved her children. There were school uniforms to wash, a house to look about, and two faces constantly in need of something, even when they were away, in school or playing in the yard at the front of the house. Sometimes Pepper's mind would remember herself, and she might wonder with a detached curiosity what became of a certain three-teeth man.

· · ·

The day it happened, the purple flowers of the tree outside Kadi-ann and Jadi-ann's window were in bloom. Mornings before school when the daylight flooding through the open curtain of the window forced their eyes open, they lay in bed watching the tree outside their window, elbowing each other every time a bird appeared. They lay this way until their mother's calls beckoned them to their knees thanking God for another morning, then to meet the cooling porridge she laid on the table for them.

But that morning was different because it was the first day of Christmas vacation, so there was no cooling porridge or the hurried rag Pepper wiped them down with. Neither of the girls liked to be wiped down, since the rag was dipped in a basin of cold water, but they knew better than to wriggle or complain, because their mother would pinch their necks. Pepper would wipe each girl separately. First the face, and then she would always wipe the inside of their ears, even if the insides looked clean, because she hated to see wax in a child's ear. To her it made a child look as if she belonged to no one. If Pepper was strict about anything, she was strict about how she sent the girls to school. When the ears were done, she would put the rag over the girls' noses for any mucus to be blown out, and then the rag was rinsed in the basin. When next the rag was wringed, it would meet the little girls' backs, stomachs, the spaces between their legs they knew to open without having to be reminded. Then the rag was rinsed again. But that morning the girls lay in bed holding their mermaid dolls and whispering a game where the bedsheets became a body of water. Later, Pepper would appear with the basin and two rags for Kadi-ann and Jadi-ann to clean themselves, and there was relief in gently handling the cold water by themselves.

People who can't afford nice things want nice things too, the holidays especially bring them about, and so Pepper agreed to sew Vernetta's Christmas church dress on the agreement that Vernetta would bring her a weekly portion of the freshwater fish her husband caught until the dress was paid off. That was why Pepper was scaling fish behind the house when Old Henry's wife came to her, tears in the old lady's eyes. Pepper wiped her hands on her apron and stood to hear what Mrs. Old Henry had to say.

But before Mrs. Old Henry showed up behind the house, Pepper was scaling the fish Vernetta brought over that morning while her mind debated how to prepare it. She knew the girls only liked fried fish when she picked out the bones and they only had to be worried with the white flesh, but she didn't have any oil and couldn't be bothered to go buy or borrow any. She wondered if Mrs. Old Henry might have a little oil she could borrow, and that was what she was waiting to ask after Mrs. Old Henry said whatever it was that carried her next door with tears in her eyes.

Who knew what stories the two little girls told themselves as they dipped the mermaid tails into the water their mother used to wash clothes. Who knew what magic, if any, they created in the worlds their mermaids inhabited. Or if mermaids fit into their world, a world where their mother sewed clothes while she drank a cup of tea and watched that they ate their dinner; they slept in the bed where their grandmother used to sleep before she died and they were afraid whenever they remembered that the bed they slept in was where their grandma used to sleep before she died.

The two mermaid dolls came in a barrel, stuffed between the clothes, rice, beans, canned foods, and various dry goods Pauline's people sent her from the States. Pauline, who lived on the other side of Old Henry, asked her sister to include two dolls in the barrel for payment to Pepper since she was short on cash when she picked up her husband's new church suit for the Christmas service.

Pauline brought over the dolls, and because she was in a generous mood, a packet of spaghetti, a can of spaghetti sauce, and a can of meatballs. She remembered that the girls were eating their dinner and Pepper was drinking a cup of tea and sewing. Pauline would tell people that the girls looked shyly at the dolls the whole time she spoke with Pepper. When the conversation started to die, she remembered what she was there for, and offered one doll to each girl. Pauline said they looked at her as though she was telling them lies.

Except for a hi and bye when they passed each other on the road, Pauline didn't talk to Pepper again until after the girls were gone. Her husband told her he saw Pepper spread on the steps in the front of her house showing everybody her business, so it was Pauline who asked Pepper for the phone numbers of her family members. She started calling around until the sister in the States offered to take Pepper.

Pauline used to see the girls holding the dolls when they followed behind Pepper to go to the shop or to drop off sewing at somebody's house. When she heard about the drowning, the part about the mermaids haunted her days and even her nights. She soon fretted away the baby weight she had been holding on to for five years. Everybody who she told the story to, and she told the story to everyone who came her way, said it wasn't her fault and had nothing to do with her because they realized a part of her felt some kind of accountability in the whole mess.

They swam those mermaids all over. In the tub their mother was washing clothes in whenever she turned her back because she forgot the soap or wanted to check on whatever she left cooking on the stove. In the buckets their mother left outside for collecting rainwater, or in rain puddles if the rain left a deep enough puddle. Living next to Old Henry, they couldn't help knowing about his tank. On the hottest days, they saw the boys Old Henry chased from his tank. Pepper had given the girls an old bucket she found in the old chicken coop behind the house. They filled it with water and for days anyone passing by could see the girls making the mermaids swim at the front of their house. Some people who passed by would smile at two identical little girls so focused on a dusty old bucket. No one would wonder at the stories they were whispering to themselves until they were gone. And people would wonder if the crack along the bucket that traveled down and ruined the possibility of it keeping water was what sent the girls to Old Henry's tank.

Because of the cement blocks, it seemed to everyone that the girls were smart enough to play in the water without getting into the tank. Recent heavy rainfall had filled the tank, bringing the water level almost to the brim. People guessed they fell in, maybe one started falling in and the other held on to her and that was how both girls fell in. This was the story people told to each other and passed down to their children as a warning. Still, dissatisfaction lurked in everybody's minds. Did those girls jump in that tank? Were the cement blocks only used as stepping-stones to climb into the tank? They didn't think they would drown? They had to know they would drown.

The part that bothered people was why when the girls were found they were only wearing their panties. Their clothes had been spread on the grass nearby. If they weren't going swimming, what was the sense in undressing? An explanation went around and it settled some people's questions: the girls were afraid of getting in trouble with Pepper if their clothes got wet. But no one who saw the girls swimming their mermaids in puddles the rain left behind in the middle of the road believed that explanation. No one who saw the girls running out of the road when the rare approaching car started to beep its horn was satisfied. No one who saw the girls with the dolls could believe that they could have common sense as far as the dolls were concerned to be worried with keeping their clothes dry. No one who saw them believed that explanation because how it was in those old-time stories, how a mermaid could sing a sweet song and turn someone into a fool was how it was with those two little girls. Maybe because they had never owned anything so good in their short lives.

BAD BEHAVIOR

Pam and Curtis brought Stacy to Jamaica because they didn't know what else to do with her. They believed that her old-time granny would straighten her out. In Brooklyn, Stacy cut her classes often, and she was caught giving a boy a blowjob in an empty classroom. They looked at the sweet little face on the body of a woman, and they were terrified of her and for her. It seemed that her breasts and ass were getting bigger every day. Often Pam would pull down Stacy's shirt to give her ass better coverage, and Stacy would groan and laugh, tucking her shirt back into her jeans. Pam wondered aloud to Curtis whether Stacy's curvy body was because of all the chicken wings she enjoyed eating from the Chinese restaurant. In America, Pam argued, chickens were injected with hormones, which could explain all the little black girls with breasts and asses before their time. Stacy refused to eat breakfast because she was never hungry in the mornings, and because the school lunch was "nasty," she was ravenous by the end of the school day. She would come home with a takeout box: pork fried rice and fried chicken wings. She ate while she did her homework—somehow, in the midst of teenage angst and man hunger, she remained a diligent student—and later she would refuse to eat dinner with her parents and little brother because she was still full. Recently, Curtis was driving on Rockaway Parkway when he saw Stacy walk out of the train station, just come from school. A man, not a boy, but a man in baggy jeans, just any old street thug, had called to his daughter, and she had actually turned around and walked back to him. They were still talking when Curtis showed up to escort Stacy home. Pam and Curtis were afraid of their fourteen-year-old daughter. Often they would tell each other that this was what America did to children. This blasted country that turned parents into children and children into parents! One need not look any further than the white people on television who asked their children what they wanted to eat for dinner. In Jamaica, children knew to respect adults, while it wasn't unusual to hear an American child call an adult by her first name. It wasn't that Jamaican children were perfect—it was that when they made mistakes, they knew to be ashamed. All children were selfish, but American ones had an easier time living for themselves.

They took their daughter to Jamaica on the pretense of a

vacation. Before they left Brooklyn, when Pam checked Stacy's suitcase, she found that her daughter had packed two
nameplate necklaces that read BAD BITCH and FLAWLESS, and
some thongs that Pam didn't know she owned. Pam left the
"flawless" necklace in the suitcase and hid the "bad bitch"
necklace and thongs. Stacy didn't seem to notice the missing
items. On the beach, she wore sunglasses and the two-piece
bathing suit she'd bought with her own money, revealing the
belly button piercing her parents didn't know she had. When
a dreadlocked man saw her sitting on the beach by herself, he
invited her to follow him to his house. She had looked into
the man's face and kissed her teeth without fear as though he
and she were size. Every day, Stacy climbed the mango tree
behind her grandma's house and then she ate several mangoes in one sitting. In the afternoons, she walked down to
the shop to buy banana chips, even though she had five un-
opened packages sitting on the dresser, because she liked that
the boy at the counter flirted with her and looked openly at
her breasts.

On the fifth day, while Stacy slept, her parents and little
brother left. A few hours later, her grandmother, Trudy,
nudged her out of bed, asking, "Yuh goin' sleep di whole
day?" She was eating the saltfish and dumplings her grandmother made for breakfast when she thought to ask about her
parents and brother. It wasn't the first morning she'd awak-
ened late to hear that they'd started the day without her. At
first, Trudy ignored her, so Stacy asked again. "Yuh nah be'ave
yuhself," her grandmother told her, speaking quietly and

carefully, "so dey lef' yuh wid me until yuh can be'ave yuh-self." Stacy behaved very badly, cussing up some bad words and throwing her breakfast on the floor, which surprised the old lady so much that all she could say was "Jesus Christ." She hadn't believed the girl was as bad as they said, and since she was lonely living in that house by herself, she'd gladly welcomed her. Stacy ran to the front of the house and looked down the road to see if they had only recently left. She knew this couldn't be the case, but she looked anyway. Then she went to the back of the house, behind the old pit toilet, so that she could cry without anyone seeing her. She bawled for a long time. She punched her fist into the walls of the long-retired pit toilet, but the pain only made her cry harder. She felt someone watching, and when she looked down, Fatty, her grandmother's mongrel dog, was looking up at her. She bent to rub Fatty's belly, which was heavy with puppies, and the dog reached up to lick the tears from her face.

Over the first two weeks after her parents left, Stacy's spirit softened. She was quieter, more inward. When she spoke to her parents on the phone, she promised that she would behave herself. But Curtis and Pam weren't ready to let Stacy back into their home. There were times they missed her—she was, after all, a sweet girl when she wanted to be, and she was the firstborn, which meant they loved her in a different—not necessarily better—way than they loved their son, Curtis Jr., a chubby ten-year-old who was an easy child. They told her that after a year, if she improved, she could come home.

• • •

Eventually, Trudy brought up Stacy's bad behavior back in New York: "Yuh such ah pretty girl fi do some ugly tings. Why yuh won' be'ave yuhself?" And Stacy had smiled and looked embarrassed because she was shy for her grandmother to know certain things about her, and yet it was a compliment to hear that she was pretty. She'd been afraid when she put her mouth on the boy's penis. Patrick was one of the most desired boys in school, and of all the other girls, he had pulled Stacy into an empty classroom, putting her hand down his pants so that she could touch his penis. This happened a few times, them kissing in empty classrooms, and one day he pushed his fingers down her jeans, and eventually she climaxed, and it was surprising and gratifying because she had never masturbated before and hadn't known that a boy's fingers could do that to her. She told one of her friends and the friend had been surprised to hear that Stacy hadn't reciprocated, and this made Stacy feel as though she'd done something wrong. She was sure that Patrick would never pull her into a classroom again, and when he did, she wanted to make it so that he wouldn't be disappointed. The first and only time, she was caught. Her parents had been furious, and they had said all kinds of things, but they hadn't asked why.

Every morning, Trudy woke her granddaughter so that she could help with the breakfast, and she would help with the other meals as well. Stacy learned to fry dumplings that were almost as good as her grandmother's, to make a nice chicken foot soup, and to bake sweet potato pudding. In New

York, Pam had done all the cooking. When Stacy started at the all-girls high school, she learned to wash her uniform by hand even though Trudy had a washing machine, because her grandmother claimed that it was the only way to ensure that a white shirt was really clean. She was distracted from boys because the relationships with her classmates were so intricate and consuming, all of them interested in befriending the foreign girl.

The mother Trudy had been was another woman. When Pam was sixteen, Trudy, acting on a tip from a neighbor, had found a love letter in one of her daughter's schoolbooks and had punched her, even slapped her face. It wasn't until Pam had become a woman with a husband and children that she could almost forgive her mother. Not all mothers could afford to be kind. When Pam had first come to America, she cleaned for a white family, and one afternoon, standing at her employer's bedroom door, she overheard the woman and her teenage daughter debate the daughter's decision to lose her virginity to her boyfriend. Pam marveled that this was a thing that could happen. She had vowed to become a better mother than Trudy. But then, without realizing until it was too late, without knowing why or how, she had failed her daughter. She had had to send her daughter to her mother, and she hoped that the old woman would be tough. Maybe, she thought, maybe the formula so many Caribbean mothers use on their daughters wasn't the worst thing. Maybe, she thought, it was sacrilege for daughters to discuss their sex lives with their mothers, and what a daughter needed was not a confidante but a woman who loved her enough to show her some of the harshness that the world was ready and able to give her.

For a long time after Pam came to America, it seemed that she was eternally in school. At first, for years, she studied on a part-time basis for her bachelor's degree. After all, she hadn't come to America to clean and cook for white people and take care of their children. After marrying Curtis, she went to school to become a registered nurse. It had taken longer than necessary because she had to attend part-time. She needed an income, so she was still cleaning for white people and taking care of their children. When Stacy was growing up, Pam was always working overtime so that they could buy a house. And when she and Curtis bought a house, she worked overtime so that they could pay the mortgage, the water bill, the electric bill, and all the other bills that came with owning a house. She'd married a man who wasn't as ambitious as she was. For years, she nagged Curtis to go to school, and for years he said that he would look about it soon but soon never came. He was a simple man when she'd met him, and she believed that he would be good to her, so she married him for something that wasn't quite love and because she was tired of struggling in America without a green card. When she met him, he made his money by cleaning for the church he attended, and though it wasn't plenty of money, he seemed contented. Now he was one of the janitors at an elementary school. If it had been up to Curtis, she and the children would have stayed in that tiny two-bedroom on Sterling Street and he wouldn't have minded. Curtis, unlike Pam, hadn't come to America for a better life. He'd left Jamaica because his mother had filed for him, and he figured that it seemed like a reasonable opportunity. Pam worked hard because she had to—what choice did she have with a husband like Curtis? If she didn't put a pot on the stove, the thought would never have occurred to him. Before she had children, she had hoped that she would see her daughter as more than a daughter, as a person with desires and her own set of truths, but it turned out that all she saw was a child who needed from her. She determined that what a daughter needed was to be fed, clothed, baptized, and protected from men. When her daughter put her mouth on that boy's penis, the question hadn't been why, but the answer had been no.

The following year, Pam, Curtis, and Curtis Jr. return to Jamaica. Pam leaves Curtis and Curtis Jr. to bring the suitcases into the house, while she goes looking for her daughter. The house is empty, so she ventures to the back, where Stacy is squatting under the mango tree, scaling a pan of fish. Pam watches her. Every time Stacy guts a fish, she throws the insides to Fatty. In New York, her daughter had certainly never cleaned fish. Of course, Pam thinks, of course my mother set her right. Unbeknownst to her, Trudy talks to her granddaughter, reasons with her. Once, they'd walked down to the shop together and because Trudy noticed that the shopkeeper's son was looking at her granddaughter as though he had plans for her, she said to him, "Tek yuh eye off mi gran'pickney. Ah no yuh get Grace pickney pregnant?" Stacy had laughed in agreement. Now she looks up, and in her excitement to greet her mother, she knocks over the pan of fish, but Fatty, who is pregnant again, is quicker than she is, grabbing a fish in her mouth and ambling off before anyone can stop her.

ISLAND

We were on the beach when the man approached us, pulling a marijuana plant out of a faded black JanSport backpack. I started to laugh. It seemed like just the kind of ridiculous caricature of a scene from a film set in Jamaica—a bare-chested Rasta man pulling the entire plant out of his bag as though only twenty minutes ago he'd lifted it from where it hung drying in an unused closet in his house. But there we were, and it was really happening. He wanted to sell to us in the aggressive way of Jamaican merchants, so that even though we hadn't shown any interest in his product, he was pulling it out of his bag and asking how much we wanted. Andrea and Tracy, true to themselves, jumped up and backed away. I'd hoped they'd relax on this trip. Who wouldn't want to smoke bud in Jamaica? And it was basically being handed to us.

I'd observed from the corner of my eyes the group of dykes sitting close by. One of them had blue dreadlocks, reminding me of a woman I'd hooked up with in New York, Jessica with the emerald hair. But what had fascinated me about her was that though she was Chinese-American, she spoke like a black woman, and it seemed to come naturally to her. We'd sat next to each other at a coffee shop in gentrified Brooklyn and hadn't talked until she was getting up to leave, and by then there was all this built-up tension. The sex had been mediocre. Besides the woman with blue dreadlocks, there were three others—they were all tattooed and pierced with partially shaved heads, that aesthetic of gay white women. I'd noticed the prettiest one among them—soft butch because of her long brown hair and black bikini—and she had looked away when she saw me looking. The next thing I knew, the dykes were crowded around the Rasta man and me, Andrea, and Tracy were leaving, and afterwards, we were passing a blunt around on a secluded area of the beach as the sun went down. I learned that they were graduate students from Chicago.

"Our friend who used to be gay is getting married to a man," the one with blue hair explained. Her friends chuckled, but had I imagined that though she smiled, there was something darker behind it?

"I'm here for a straight wedding, too," I told them. "Tia and I fooled around, but she would never admit that there is a gay bone in her body."

They clucked knowingly.

They wanted to hear about my life in New York, which made me feel self-conscious. I always wanted to impress queer women, and people tend to have naïve expectations of life in New York. I started talking about a club I'd been to. A woman I'd met on Tinder was DJing, which was how I made it onto the VIP list. All night long, people were saying that the singer Shirley was on the dance floor and it seemed that everyone but me had seen her, until I went to use the bathroom and she held the door open for me. The woman with the blue dreadlocks was actually Mexican-American, so I'd forgiven her the hair offense, until she said, "Who's Shirley? Sorry, I don't listen to pop music."

When the talk of their dissertations and the bliss of the Caribbean sun started to bore me, I got up to leave. But there had been a transcendent moment when the blunt had been in my hand, and I looked around at four other women who were not yet thirty and seemed at peace with something as primal and contentious as desire for other women. I was happy and I was gay, and it occurred to me that both of these things could happen at the same time. "I'll see you ladies later," I said, but I was looking at the one in the black bikini. Her name was Jen.

I found Andrea and Tracy eating in the dining room. Andrea had an entire fish laid out in front of her, and Tracy was sipping a thick, fragrant soup. Even though I couldn't reasonably hold it against them, I was annoyed that they'd gone to dinner without me. I'd only been away for maybe thirty minutes and they were already carrying on without me. I knew

that if it had been one of them who was delayed, we'd have
waited. But this wasn't always the case for me. I would do a
gay thing, and when I came back both of their faces were
posed at me in an ordinary way, but I couldn't help wondering what they had said about me behind my back.

"You made some new friends," Tracy said, smiling, but I
could see that she was studying me carefully.

"Yeah, they're from Chicago—they're graduate students,"
I explained. "They've also come for a wedding."

"A gay wedding in Jamaica?" Andrea looked confused.

"No, it's a straight wedding."

"Oh, that makes more sense."

I'd always wanted to go to Jamaica as a tourist—to see the
island as an outsider. Who doesn't want to, at a certain point,
be pampered in her own home? It's why, I suspect, my mother
used to ask us to bring her a glass of water even though the
kitchen was the next room over, and why she would sit in the
bathtub after a long day at work and call one of us to scrub
her back. Yet when I told my mother that I was going to a
destination wedding in Jamaica, spending all that money for
a couple I'd known in Madison when I was in law school, she
hissed her teeth and asked if I didn't have better use for my
money. We'd left Jamaica when I was a child, and we'd gone
back only to visit family.

But I was optimistic—here was the trip I'd always wanted
to take with my friends, and finally it was happening. And I
needed to travel. I wasn't over Allison. After I graduated,

she'd moved back to New York with me, but it was all drama with her, the persistent gaslighting and the fact that she was always the victim as no one, not even I, who claimed to love her, could understand her trauma. As a girl, there'd been a man who lived next door, who invited her over affectionately and then forcefully, and it had gone on for years. When she announced that she was moving back to the Midwest, that Brooklyn wasn't her speed, and that I reminded her of her mother since we shared the same horoscope sign, I hadn't begged her to stay. I was in love but I was tired.

Tracy and Andrea were both excited about our trip. They were still living in the Midwest pursuing their degrees, and I would call from my apartment in Brooklyn and they would tell me how the college town hadn't changed—the undergraduates were still plentiful and boozy on a Saturday night, the black eligible men were few—and then they would gush over how lucky I was to be living in New York. And so we all had our separate reasons for fleeing to Jamaica. We looked forward to the buffets of tropical fruit—we would, we pledged, eat mangoes by the half dozen. We wanted to sit by the Caribbean Sea, our legs naked and warmed by the sun. We talked about a man Andrea was interested in—a man in her department who was giving her mixed signals. We talked about a man who'd asked Tracy to dinner but she was unsure whether she was interested. I offered advice. Neither of them asked about my romantic life. Sometimes, I thought they were just no longer interested in our friendship, but then I reminded myself that they'd made a point of keeping in touch. Still, when I hugged them, I would wonder if they felt uncomfortable. I questioned whether they thought I was destined for hell or if I had, in some way, opened up their minds to other ways of living. But really, I had no idea what to think.

When we arrived at the hotel room, although we'd never discussed sleeping arrangements, I noticed that when we sat down to figure out our evening plans, I was sitting on one bed by myself and they were sitting on the other bed. Later that night, they crawled into bed together but I only registered this through tipsy eyes, and so it wasn't until the next morning that it stung.

Red bougainvillea framed the grounds of the hotel, those prideful flowers, and meanwhile Brian, the best man, light-skinned and pretty, decided in his head that I was interested in him. I could tell that he was the species of black man who believed that he was a catch because he was college educated, hadn't ever been to jail or sold drugs in the hood, and as far as the world was concerned and fuck the fact that it exoticized him, he had a big dick. A man like that wasn't about to let a black woman forget that he was her ideal and the fact that his ex-girlfriend, who he had been briefly engaged to, had been a white woman. Over drinks, he tossed his Ivy League education and job in finance my way, mentioning it casually but making eye contact with me every now and then to see whether this information impressed me. All of us who had come for the wedding had met in the bar, reacquainting or meeting for the first time. There were a little over thirty of us, and energy was high because here we were in paradise. Brian was talking about a restaurant he had gone to with an ex-girlfriend, and a few minutes later, Beyoncé and Jay Z were seated at the table next to them. Tracy and Andrea, and Isaiah and Tia, our two friends to be married, as well as everyone else gathered around looked impressed, but I almost rolled my eyes. When I left to get another drink, Mr. Wall Street showed up next to me, flashing his well-attended teeth, and meanwhile I was wondering exactly what it was that he wanted from me. I assumed that it was a little vacation sex because he had the misfortune of traveling to a beautiful locale during the off-season, that he was without a girlfriend, and that the woman he was sleeping with in New York, a pretty little young light-skinned thing or a naïve white girl, couldn't be taken on the trip without assuming that it meant something more than it was.

"Has anyone ever told you that you could pass for Lisa Bonet's little sister?" he asked.

I laughed. "Someone once told me that I'm Lisa Bonet with Queen Latifah titties."

He grinned, taking a long sip of his drink.

"Of course, this was before my breast reduction."

I could tell that he wasn't quite sure how to respond, so I continued, "Which Lisa Bonet do you mean?"

"Which Lisa Bonet?"

"Yeah. Are we talking *Cosby Show* Lisa Bonet or married-to-a-*Game-of-Thrones*-babe-warrior Lisa Bonet?"

He laughed. "I still haven't seen *Game of Thrones*. What are you drinking?"

"Pineapple juice with rum."

"I've never had that combo before."

"Yeah? A woman I dated put me on to it." He was visibly surprised, which I loved. Some men tried to brush it off as though they'd known all along. I reminded them of their aunts who believed in incense, shea butter, and head wraps—the type of woman who was always less conforming than their mothers, who wore pantyhose to church on Sundays. They admired these aunts, these pariahs and poets who kept relationships and children with men they weren't married to. But unlike their aunts, I'd gone too far. I liked it best when they couldn't hold their disbelief, because who were they to assume anything about me? One Jamaican man in Brooklyn, just someone who had approached me on the street, told me, "Yuh too pretty to be wid women." Brian and I talked for a bit longer, during which he asked the obligatory question of whether I also dated men, and when I said that I no longer did, I could see that his interest waned and he scanned the room to see who his other options were.

He was gone by the time Tia showed up next to me. "So Brian found out that you don't date men, huh?" We laughed and turned to look at the other woman he was now in the process of wooing—a cousin of Tia's with long extensions, who was wearing one of those extraordinarily low-cut dresses that small-breasted women can get away with. I'd had a crush on Tia when we were in law school together. She had a way about her that made it seem like she slept with women. I'd even assumed that much until she introduced me to her boy-

friend when I bumped into them on campus. One night after
we shared two bottles of wine, the both of us newly single
and commiserating, I dared myself to tell her that when I
first met her I thought that she was gay and that I had had a
crush on her. We'd laughed about it as though it was a silly
thing I'd said because I'd had too much to drink. But then a
few weeks later, before Tia had gotten together with Isaiah,
we'd fooled around. We hadn't had sex exactly but we'd
come close, and afterwards she was apologetic because she'd
been the one to kiss me. She wasn't sure, she said, that it was
anything more than a thing she wanted to try, and because I
didn't want to be something someone tried and more so because it seemed that Allison and I would be getting back together, we agreed to be friends.

When Isaiah came over and put his arm over my shoulder, I shuddered without meaning to. I'd never gotten used to
him—he'd played football in college and was one of those
beefy, touchy types. It mattered greatly to him and Tia that
they were both Chicagoans who had gone to the same elementary school when they were little and had met in graduate school in Wisconsin, but it was far too sentimental and
irrelevant a story to matter to anyone else, because they were
so mismatched. Tia was a sensitive, artsy type who had somehow stumbled into law school because her middle-class upbringing had determined this path. I imagined that in five
years she would quit law to work for an art nonprofit, when
she wasn't caring for her and Isaiah's children. Whenever I
imagined them having sex, it always began with Isaiah lifting

Tia and throwing her into bed. I never thought they would
date for more than a few months—just long enough to realize
their incompatibility.

"So when are you getting married?" Isaiah asked, now
squeezing my shoulder. It was obvious that he was joking,
that what he meant was that he wanted everyone to be as
happy as he and Tia were, but I couldn't let him have it. I
couldn't be nice because nice to me was too passive, so I said,
"And subscribe to a system of patriarchy?" Beside him, Tia
rolled her eyes. In two days, she would make a beautiful
bride. She was one of those undercover beauties who would
change out of her jeans and T-shirt into something glamor-
ous and you'd wonder how you'd managed to overlook her
in the first place. Once, drunkenly, Isaiah asked when I was
going to join them in bed. We were outside a bar, smoking.
He had lit my cigarette for me and afterwards he stood looking at me for too long a moment, and so I knew what was
coming. Before that night, I'd suspected that I didn't like Isaiah, but afterwards I determined that I didn't like him. I knew
that Tia never told him about us. I could tell that she was
confused enough about it to keep it to herself for a long time,
maybe as long as forever. It always seemed to me that Tia was
one of those women who might have been a lesbian, or at
least open to desiring women, if life had opened up the possibility and she had welcomed or at least fallen into it. It occurred to me and still occurs to me that something like that
could have happened to me. I might have married a man in a
destination wedding in Jamaica if life hadn't taken over with

a cloud of mystery to offer me another direction. It's more than being in the right place at the right time. It's more nebulous than that.

In New York, I'd gotten into the habit of sleeping with women I couldn't take seriously. It was either that, or gain twenty pounds from overeating, or take up cocaine or something, anything to take the edge off. One of the women, too young for me at twenty-three, started to cry when we saw each other on the street after I'd ignored her calls and texts for weeks. "I'm sorry," I called after her, crossing the street to get away because it would have been crueler to tell her that I would never be able to love her. I continued glancing behind me for the rest of the afternoon—not sure if it was her spirit or my conscience that was taunting me.

I'd met Allison in a coffee shop. It was far enough from downtown that graduate students had taken claim. The first time I went in to meet a classmate, I stood for a long moment looking at the menu written in chalk that hung high above my head. I hardly ever went to coffee shops. I liked to study in private and I hated the taste of coffee. Allison watched my face carefully from behind the counter, smiling a little smile as though she wanted to laugh at customers like me who deliberated for a long time before they ordered something as basic as a chai latte. I kept going back, sometimes with friends but mostly alone. I kept ordering chai lattes for three months before Allison said, "We should get a drink soon. I'm assuming you drink? You look like you drink." How had she known that? Was it the long dreads hanging down my back? The big hoop earrings and Cosby sweater I'd worn that day? Was it because I was black?

Slowly, I learned things about Allison too. She was a graduate student in the poetry program, she drank something called a matcha latte, and she liked cotton candy colors. Between customers, she read poetry books at the counter or drew faces of imaginary people in a little black notebook. When I told her that I wrote poetry yet I had declined a funded poetry MFA program for law school, her eyes widened. "I'd love to read your work someday," she said, and I could tell that she meant it.

The evening we met for a drink, I was just beginning to question my sexuality. I looked around the bar and made eye contact with a black woman I recognized from around town. I saw us as she must have seen us, but now I know that I projected what I wanted her to see: two women, one of them almost the same coffee-with-cream shade as her and the other with long, messy blonde hair hanging around her face, on a date.

With Allison, it had been like learning a new language. There was a different vocabulary to dating women. She showed me where and how to position my body during sex. I even learned to love coffee. But we were so different. She was certain that poetry could change the world, but I wasn't so sure. I knew that she would respect me if I quit law school and published a chapbook. Her parents were intellectuals who never had to fret about money, not like my mother had to, and Allison was the same. There was an entitled, naïve way about her that I kept forgiving. She was the kind of white person who would never let me forget my blackness—she would detail oppressions to me as though I hadn't lived them.

"I know I'm black," I told her once. "You don't have to keep reminding me."

"Why are you so resistant to love?" she'd asked, which was an entirely different argument, but she couldn't understand that.

Tia and Isaiah convinced everyone to go to the dance-hall-themed party in one of the resort's entertainment rooms. I'd spent too much of my life subjected to men rubbing against me as a masculine gesture of dancing, but just as I was about to bow out, Tia gently placed her hand against my back as though she could read my mind. The room was darkly lit, and, accompanied by a Beenie Man song, I could almost smell the sex in the air. Those of us women who had traveled without dates danced together, but eventually everyone besides me peeled off as men approached them. Andrea and Tracy were dancing with two red-haired brothers from the UK, who kept exchanging glances at what I imagined was the possibility of both getting laid on the same night. I could see Tracy being game—she had a way of sleeping with men because they'd called her beautiful. A dog had bitten her right cheek when she was a little girl, and even now that the scar had faded, she slathered the area with foundation before appearing in public. Andrea had a face like a baby with her fat cheeks, but she was more cynical than she looked. A man had to earn her pussy. I swayed alone in the midst of strangers, shaking my head at the men who approached me. A few feet away, Tia was rubbing her ass against Isaiah's crotch. I tried to catch her eyes, but she was looking past me.

I'd stepped outside when Brian approached me.

"Tired of dancing?" he asked.

"I just needed a moment. It's hot in there."

"I can understand that."

We walked down to the beach. As we sat facing the water, I remember that we talked about all kinds of things. He'd voted for Obama but was disappointed by the presidency. He thought Obama should do more for black people. He'd dated his high school girlfriend throughout college, and was disappointed that she hadn't waited a little longer for him to grow up. She'd married a white man in graduate school. He hadn't eaten meat for the past ten years. He thought that with time maybe Allison and I would get back together.

"You're different than I thought you were," I told Brian, as we were walking to his room. He tried to hold my hand, but I wouldn't let him. Afterwards, I made him high-five me, which made us both laugh.

On my walk back to the dance party, the sea air felt good, calming. I wasn't thinking about Brian or Allison or anyone else. I was remembering a day from my childhood when my father drove to the sea and left me in the car to go into a house, which belonged to one of his extramarital lovers—though I didn't know who she was at the time. When they came out of the house together, she handed me a cup filled with cherries that were cold, as though she'd just taken them from the fridge.

There were a few dancers straggling, and Isaiah broke from a conversation with his cousin about the upcoming NFL season to tell me that Tia, Andrea, and Tracy were in the bathroom.

"I had one in my early twenties, but I would never tell Isaiah," Tia was saying, too loudly. She was a confessional drunk. I'd walked in just as another woman was leaving, and because a wall separated the door from the sinks, she couldn't see me.

"You think it would bother him?" Tracy asked. I imagined that she was looking in the mirror, smoothing her foundation to keep the scar hidden.

"I just don't think it's his business."

"You really believe that she left with Brian?" Andrea asked.

"It wouldn't surprise me," Tracy said.

"Why wouldn't it surprise you?" Tia asked. "From what I saw, she couldn't tolerate him. And isn't she a lesbian?"

"I don't know what she is," Tracy said.

They laughed. I left as quietly as I came.

Andrea, Tracy, and I could talk about everything—the length and width of a man's penis, how we had failed our mothers and how they had failed us, the nitty-gritty of being a woman, black, and Caribbean, and everything else in between. The stuff at the back of our throats or buried even deeper. But we could never talk about Allison. When I discovered that I could find myself in love with a woman, whenever I thought about the two of us holding hands in public in that Midwestern town, I only worried about Tracy and Andrea seeing us before I could come out to them. And when I finally told them, with the simplicity of "Allison and I are dating," they admitted that they'd known, they'd noticed our intimacy. It was clear that it had been a conversation between them, and it wasn't that they were cruel or unsupportive, but I had thought that they might appear more interested in the most interesting thing that had ever happened to me. But I couldn't think about that just yet—I could only think about the relief of telling them. Afterwards, I cried in the shower.

There is so much you want to tell your friends. You want to tell them when happiness looks different than you ever imagined it could—that what you had been waiting for, how you were expecting love to feel and to look, doesn't compare to another version that is altogether a surprise and nevertheless, unbeknownst to you, what you had been waiting for. You want to tell them that the first time a woman kisses you, you are deflated and ecstatic by how normal it is. You want them to ask about the sex—even though at first you don't know how you feel about it. You want to explain because to tell is sometimes the only way to understand. It had been like being unwrapped—your soul and your body being reduced to their most essential hungers. You hadn't thought about God or blasphemy or what your mother would say; your mind, your being, had been elevated to a place where none of that mattered. It had been freeing to give in to love like that. I hadn't imagined that I could be that brave. And this, this triumph, is a thing you want to say to your friends.

The summer I realized I was a lesbian, I thought about my island. What, I asked myself, if we built islands around ourselves, because it's no sin to be self-sufficient? I even tried to write a poem about it. It was about independence and loneliness, protection and fear—the latter I tried to deny for a long time. I tried to make the imagery beautiful—the landscape lush, and the sea a color from my childhood when we still lived in Jamaica and my father used to take us to the beach on Sunday mornings. I returned to the poem two months ago, when I finally quit my job at the law firm and found an administrative job I was overqualified for, but which freed up my evenings to write. But eventually and repeatedly the poem would come to a standstill because language betrayed me every time. I didn't know how to articulate the face my mother made when I told her that I'd gone against everything and found myself in love with a woman. First, I wanted to be a writer, and then I discovered that I was a lesbian, and after everything, attending law school and all those years of sleeping with men, those desires still found me in the end. There seemed to be no island that could hold me then—no place seemed far or big or safe enough. Yes, I could leave, could wrap blankets of protection around myself, but I would remember my loved ones and what they were thinking of me. The silence would be lonely.

· · ·

The day after the dance party, Andrea and Tracy came looking for me. I imagine that they'd tried our room as well as the
dining areas and bars before they came to the beach. After
lunch, I'd gone back to our room to take a nap, leaving them
to flirt with one of the waiters, who joked, though I suspected that he was serious, that he was looking for an American woman to marry. Later, I would learn that they'd wanted
to know if I was coming with them to a reggae concert put
on by a Bob Marley impersonator. Jen and I were sitting on
the beach, and she had been talking about her dissertation—
she was going on in a way that made me realize that she
wanted to impress me. We were holding each other's gaze,
and she was talking about suicide and women poets, women
who to her had been casualties of the time during which they
lived, and meanwhile I was wondering why it seemed that
the only queer women who pursued me were white intellec-
tual types, ones who spent too much time in their own heads.
I'd had bad luck with this kind of woman—overly sensitive,
entitled despite their secular humanist liberal thinking.
When the conversation lapsed and we were looking toward
the sea, I turned back toward her, thinking of a question I
could ask that would keep the conversation going, but before
I could speak, Jen kissed me. It was only a few seconds before
I pulled away, my fear overwhelming my desire until I remembered that I was at a resort. I'd heard of people killed in
Jamaica for less—even the suspicion of their sexuality mark-
ing them for a violent visitation. I looked behind me to see
Andrea and Tracy walking away from us. I knew that they'd

seen us. Before I could think what to do, I jumped up and caught up to them.

"We didn't want to interrupt," Tracy said. She was smiling, but I could tell that she was uncomfortable. She was the worldliest of us—she'd traveled, she'd had foreign lovers—and yet she couldn't handle this. Andrea looked as though she was making a conscious effort to fix her face in a pleasing way. She was the softer of the two, reflecting a strict, upper-middle-class upbringing in Barbados. When I'd come out to them, my voice had become the texture it changes to when I'm holding back from crying. Andrea had told me, "I think it takes strength to be vocal about something like that." Tracy had warned me against telling my mother.

They'd never seen me physically affectionate with a woman before, though. Something about how they were standing together now, how one of them could speak for the both of them, and there was as well the fact that they weren't going to address the thing they'd seen, made me feel that in that moment the only option I had was to walk away. So I went back to Jen, and afterwards we met her friends in the bar, and by then I was okay, I wasn't thinking about Andrea and Tracy and why my sexuality was an elephant in the room of our friendship or what they had thought when they saw me kissing another woman, because I didn't care. The piña coladas were strong, and I was distracted by my horniness and the knowledge that Jen and I would fuck when we got to the room she shared with her friends. We did, and I'd never had sex like that before—it was as though it being transgressive made it hotter. Maybe we both felt as though we had something to prove. That's the only way I can explain it.

When I got back to my room, Andrea and Tracy were sleeping. It was 2 a.m. and I still felt very much awake. I looked out the window for what seemed a long time, listening to the sea kiss the shore as though it could tell me its secrets. I whispered a poem about women who loved women, mermaids, who lived at the bottom of the sea. I was too tired to write down the words, and in the morning I could only remember the images evoked—women with hair the colors of coral, with tails of emerald and topaz, those bare-breasted creatures that were both human and animal. In the shower, I remembered that later that day I would have to wear white—we all would. It was one of those trendy new things people were doing at weddings. I'd been annoyed having to go out and look for a white dress, a color I never wore, but right then it seemed that I could sit through a hundred white weddings. Because I have a habit of talking to myself, I said out loud what I would have said if I had friends interested, eager to hear about my night. I said, "I just fucked a woman in Jamaica," and then I dried off and, still smiling from the memory of skin on skin, eventually drifted off to sleep.

MERMAID RIVER

The sign read, WELCOME TO MERMAID RIVER and in smaller print, "No swimming, the rocks are sharp," but my grandmother remembered when the river was just a river. Nobody called it any name or took photos in front of it, and the rocks were sharp but it wasn't anything to keep anyone from swimming. When my grandmother was a girl, the river used to be fat. The days I sat with her across from Mermaid River, it was thinned down and half dried up. And the stones were sharper, angrier than my grandmother remembered them to be. As if the river rebelled when the resort wanted to stretch and the river and the surrounding land was bought up. The river became Mermaid River, and what wasn't bush to be chopped down were houses where country people lived. The houses were torn down, replaced by vacation beachside cottages. But I haven't seen Mermaid River in years, not since I left Jamaica. I only have my memories to go on.

These days, I request fried plantain between two pieces of bread for breakfast. Sometimes I ask for scrambled eggs on the side. Or an egg sandwich with fried plantain on the side. I always drink tea. The cereal boxes sit on top of the fridge, barely touched. They are the sugary kind I often see advertised on the television. My mother bought them four years ago as one of many introductions to America. Sometimes after she's put my breakfast in front of me and I sit eating alone, my eyes will catch on the boxes sitting on top of the fridge and it will occur to me to throw them out. They must be expired by now. But I never do, I always forget, and they almost seem to belong in our kitchen.

My first morning in this country, I ate the bowl of cold cereal and drank the glass of orange juice my mother put in front of me, and my stomach cramped and pained and finally I vomited. The night before, sleeping in my new bed, all of it felt strange, as though I had stepped out of my skin and was watching myself from outside myself. When I was a little boy, I used to show off to my classmates that my mother was in America and she would soon send for me. But it became a story that seemed far off, less true, almost as though it belonged to someone else, so I stopped telling it. That first night, the woman who resembled a woman I used to know— because that's how my mother seemed in the early days— showed me to my room. She opened a closet and showed me new clothes. She rubbed her hands against the dresser, pulling out drawers to reveal new socks and underwear. She explained that the entire bedroom set was new. In the woman's face, I recognized the roundness of my grandmother's face.

My second morning in this country, my mother asked what my grandmother usually gave me for breakfast. I didn't tell her porridge, which my grandmother prepared every school day, ignoring my complaints. My grandmother believed porridge was "proper food" for learning, since it was the kind of meal to keep a belly full until lunchtime. But I hated how full cornmeal porridge left me. I liked to run to school and it interfered with my speed. I also disliked the lumps and the fact that porridge always made me need to go to the bathroom in the middle of my morning classes. I hated shitting in school, because if you took too long somebody would always take notice of it and ask what you were doing, and then everyone in the class would start laughing.

Instead, I told my mother what my grandmother made on weekends, and since then I've basically eaten the same meal every weekday morning. The exception is the pancakes with syrup my mother prepares from a box on weekends—another introduction to America that I dislike. I would prefer plantain and bread and eggs, but I don't want her to feel bad. My mother worries what I will eat when I start college next fall. She says if I can get a little hot plate in my dorm, she will ship me plantains if I end up somewhere where I can't find them. I tell her she doesn't have to worry about that. I tell her I will eat American food when I have to.

I have on my coat, my hat, and I'm pulling on my gloves

when my mother walks down the stairs. She has rollers in her hair, and she's wearing the lavender nightgown. Months ago, when she stood in front of the nightgown rack at the department store, my mother was running her fingers along the pink version of the lavender nightgown. She asked me which one she should get, and since the pink reminded me that there was already too much pink in her closet, I picked the lavender one. Not long after, my mother was drinking a cup of tea while I ate my breakfast. When she got up to wash the breakfast dishes, my eyes were pulled to the back of her nightgown. It took me a moment to realize that I was looking at blood. And it took me another moment to realize it was probably period blood. I quickly turned my face away, begging my mother to see the blood herself because I didn't know how to voice those kinds of things to her. I heard her walk up the stairs, and before I left for school she had changed into another nightgown. Whenever she wears the lavender nightgown, I always remember the blood. Sometimes I look for evidence, the dull imprint of an old stain. There isn't any. My mother comes over to put some money in my hand, as she does every Monday morning since she knows I like a beef patty and a cream soda from the Jamaican restaurant after school. She also gives me the letter to show my teachers. I fold it without looking at it and put it in my coat pocket. Then she is wrapping her arms around me and whispering a quick prayer because she watches on the news the ways in which America can swallow black sons. She still worries, even though I've done well in Brooklyn for so long already.

Last night it snowed but only left a dusting. I'm watching

where my boots make prints in the snow. The thing I hate most about winter, besides the cold, snow, and extra clothes, is how dark the mornings are. Because there isn't light shining through my window, I stay in bed longer. I'm always tired until spring comes. The first year, I explained how tired I was and my mother thought maybe I had worms so she bought a special drink for me. The drink was meant to clean me out, which is why my mother asked me if I saw any worms when I used the bathroom. I told her I didn't see anything, and because she asked when my stepfather and I were eating dinner, he started to choke because he was laughing so hard, and it took him a long time to finally say, "Why are you asking the man his business for?"

There is an old woman in a wheelchair waiting at the bus stop, smoking a cigarette with gloved fingers. There are also the regulars, a mother with six children huddled up next to her. All of them look exactly like each other and nothing like her. The oldest boy helps the mother huddle the smaller ones, since her arms are busy holding the smallest one. All their names start with "Jah"—the mother is calling their names because the bus is pulling up. "Jahzalia. Jahmalia. Jahmajesty. Jahmarie. Jahzal. Jahdan." The oldest boy is hauling the stroller onto the bus and the mother calls the names of all her children, worried that she will lose one of them. The eyes of everyone on the bus are forced wide open because the mother is loud and everybody is wondering at those names and all those children.

The bus stops at the L train station and most of us, including the oldest Jah and I, get off the bus. But before he gets off, just before the bus doors open, he hollers bye to his brothers and sisters, and his mother pulls him up to her to kiss his cheek, smashing the youngest one between them. It is loud and very dramatic, even the bus driver is looking through his rearview mirror. The family does this every morning, as if they don't live in the same house and see each other on a daily basis. Then the youngest is crying and the mother is holding him up to the window so he can see the brother who is standing on the sidewalk and waving one last goodbye.

On the subway platform, the conductor speaks on the intercom, asking people to please let go of the doors. He says that another train is pulling up across the platform in two minutes, he says people are causing a delay and endangering themselves, but nobody pays him any mind. One lady was holding the doors open for a whole group of people, including me. Now a man is holding the doors open for the last stragglers.

Every morning the same old lady walks up and down the train car, preaching and giving tracts to anyone who will take them from her. She seems to always pick the fullest car, the last one, weaving her way through and around people and never bothering to break her sermon to say "Excuse me." After preaching, she prays for us and then she breaks into a hymn. The woman next to me kisses her teeth and says it is too early for all of this. Two girls, maybe two years younger than me, are leaning against the doors and laughing into each other, probably because the singing is so bad. The old lady tries to give a tract to a couple with dreadlocks but the man takes one look at the tract and says, "A white Jesus you a gi mi? Mi no bother wid nuh white Jesus." The woman he is with laughs. Most everyone else is folded into himself or herself, sleep still in their eyes because they are holding on to the last free moments before work or school.

I feel the letter in my coat pocket. Since I put it there, I haven't forgotten its invisible weight. I can imagine the tidiness of my mother's handwriting and the polite way of her words.

When I was little, my grandmother and I lived in the house I was born in. The bed my mother used to sleep in when she was a girl was the same bed she gave birth in, a bed I would claim as my own for the eight years my mother left me with my grandmother. My placenta and umbilical cord were buried under either the ackee tree or the breadfruit tree. My grandfather buried them deep so no dog could get to them, but he died when I was still a baby and my grandmother couldn't remember which tree it was. She always wanted to say it was the ackee tree but she really wasn't sure.

My name would have been Sylvia if I turned out to be a girl or Roy, after my father, if I turned out to be a boy. But when my mother pushed me out, my grandmother said that for a moment no one spoke and then the midwife, a woman with aging eyes, asked, "A light 'im light so?" No one who had seen how dark my father was would have asked that. "Samson," my grandmother said. "We a go call 'im Samson." My grandmother said she looked at my albino skin and knew I would have to be strong. That's why she named me Samson instead of after my father, who she called a "cruff" whenever his name came up. Because the labor pains silenced my mother and my grandfather wasn't interested in what they named me if it wasn't after him, no one argued with my grandmother. My name is Samson Roy Johnson.

When I lived with my grandmother, she used to take me with her down to Mermaid River. But I soon became tired of sitting around while she and the other women took care of business—selling the food they prepared, talking people's business, and whatever else old women did that bored me. I was freed when my grandmother started leaving me at the house of a woman who watched children, and then I started school. After that, I hardly bothered to make it down to Mermaid River, and then when I went of my own accord, it was because of what Roger Boxx said.

A man went mad down in Porus and chopped his wife with a machete, which was how Roger Boxx came to be in my class, since his people took him and his little sister to live with them. Everyone had heard about the woman who was chopped. My grandmother and I were eating fried fish and watching the evening news. She paused from picking a fish-bone out of her teeth to say "Jesus," almost whispering and elongating the word, in the way she did whenever she heard something painful and surprising or, sometimes, miraculous.

Roger Boxx was the shortest boy in our class. The Monday he arrived he took over from Clement Richards, who had been the shortest boy in the class but made up for his height with his voice, which sounded like he was copying after his father, who was a Seventh-day Adventist minister. Nobody paid Clement Richards's height any mind because they were invested in the way his voice sounded, in the highs and lows, the drama of it. Roger Boxx didn't seem to have anything about him to level out his height, so nobody paid him any mind. He took up a space next to those of us who were never invited to play cricket. Silently, except when it came time to cheer, we watched the games from the edge of the field.

After a week or so in our class, Roger Boxx and I were paired up as spelling partners. As soon as he sat down after pushing his desk next to mine, he told me that he had a Game Boy at home. I told him I had a three-legged dog named Delilah, who ate the pears that fell from our pear tree. We became inseparable.

I remember how one time Roger Boxx said that he wanted to see Delilah but when we got to my house, she was nowhere to be found. This was because, as I suspected about the Game Boy, I didn't have a three-legged pear-eating dog named Delilah. In fact, a man who lived down the road owned a three-legged pear-eating dog he called Trouble. The first time I asked about the dog's name, the man told me Delilah since he knew my name was Samson. I didn't confess any of this to Roger Boxx. We walked around the yard calling out Delilah's name, and I told Roger that sometimes Delilah walked all over the district and then she might come home with somebody's fowl in her mouth.

This was how Roger Boxx and I, tired of looking for Delilah, came to be playing marbles in the front yard when he looked up and asked, "Who is dat ole woman?" I looked up quickly to see who was walking into the yard and my mind got stuck on the word "ole," when I saw that he was talking about my grandmother. I never thought of her as old until he said it. Maybe because she raised me as if she was my mother since my own mother had been in New York for eight years already, working and making a way so that she could send for me. Or it could have been because my grandmother was big and tall, and even with gray hair she never seemed weak to me. Old meant weak to me then. The word surprised me, offended me, and put a fire under my tail, and so I decided that since my grandmother was old, I had a responsibility to help her more.

I get off at Broadway Junction. The preaching woman gets off too, hauling two big bags with her. Just before the train stopped, she abruptly ended the hymn, gave everybody a last word about Jesus coming again and getting our lives right, and quickly stuffed the tracts and Bible into one of her bags. We go up the stairs and then the morning crowd swallows her. I follow the crowd that gets on the down escalator and walk a little way to the stairs that lead underground to the A and C train platform. The A train is pulling off but that's okay. It's really the C I need to get on.

I sit next to a young couple sleeping on each other. It's the only free seat. The girl's legs are spread out across the guy's lap, his arms are wrapped around her, and they look to be completely lost in sleep. Across from me, a woman is looking into a mirror and putting on her entire face. My mother's voice comes into my head, so I smile. She would call the couple sleeping and the woman putting on her makeup on the train "slack." She would be horrified. She would say that Americans don't have any shame, and she would warn me, "Please, Samson, I didn't bring you to this country to take up them ways."

The day after Roger Boxx called my grandmother "old," instead of running off early to watch the cricket games in the schoolyard before school, I stayed behind. After I had eaten my porridge, washed my face, brushed my teeth, and put on my school uniform, I stood behind my grandmother in the kitchen with my hands in my khaki pants pockets. Standing around was the quickest way to become involved in whatever needed to be done around the house. "Here," my grandmother said. She bumped into me as she turned around in our small kitchen. "Yuh look like yuh wan' someting fi do." She gave me a pan filled with big pieces of coconut to cut into the little pieces she used to make coconut drops. That morning, she had thrown coconuts against a big rock behind our house because it was the way she could bust a coconut open. I'd heard the coconuts being flung while I ate my porridge.

When I got to school, Roger Boxx and the other boys, who nobody wanted on their cricket teams, were watching the last minutes of the game. Roger held his arms up to me as if to say, "Where were you?" I only shook my head, because explaining I had willingly stayed behind to help my grandmother cook wouldn't make any sense to him. I took my place next to him and we watched the rest of the game together.

After school, I told Roger Boxx that I couldn't play marbles because I had to help my grandmother. He looked at me as if I wasn't making any sense to him. After I walked out of the schoolyard, I turned around to see that he was playing football with a marble. I couldn't see the marble from the distance I was standing, for all I knew he could have been kicking a small stone, but I knew it was a marble because we played football that way sometimes. I almost went back to play with him. I'd told him a half lie. I didn't have to help my grandmother and she wasn't expecting me. My plan was to go down to Mermaid River to help with the selling and, when the sun began to set, the packing up of the leftovers and bringing it all back home.

In front of a yellow house was a tree and under the tree were three women standing huddled close to each other. I saw my grandmother before she noticed me. A big-boned tall woman, she was hard to miss. She was picking at something wrapped in a piece of foil, and then she, Mrs. Angie, and Mrs. Wright were laughing loudly, the kind of laugh that made their whole bodies dance. For a moment it seemed as though the woman laughing as if she didn't have one fret in the whole world wasn't the same woman who quarreled with me. Then my grandmother saw me and I saw myself in her eyes, a twelve-year-old boy prone to trouble since I sometimes didn't know what to do with myself. She started walking quickly toward me and I could see the questions in her face. She wanted to hear what happened, what trouble I had gotten into, since I never made it down to Mermaid River after school.

"Wah 'appen, Samson?" my grandmother asked, when she was close enough to call out to me.

"Nothin'." I shrugged my shoulders.

My grandmother stood in front of me wearing an old faded church dress and an old purse, the handles of which were tied around her waist. I knew the purse was where she kept the money she made from sales and the mints she sucked on when she felt for something in her mouth. I grew up hearing her say, "Mi feel fah something" and then she would look for the purse so she could suck on a red-and-white-striped mint. I hadn't seen the purse in some months and I missed it because I used to take money when I wanted to buy a suck-suck at the shop, or a mint when I too felt for something in my mouth. I had been taking money and mints from that purse my entire childhood and I always suspected my grandmother knew, but when she finally caught on she said, "O Lawd, O Jesus, O heaven cum down an fill mi soul, di bwoy a thief fram mi," and then she started keeping the purse somewhere in her bedroom. Although it had occurred to me to look for it, I hadn't built up the ambition, especially since the last time I went into my grandmother's bedroom to look for something she hid from me, I hit upon the pail she used in the nights when she couldn't make it to the bathroom. She had forgotten to take the pail out that morning and it occurred to me that I was looking at the entire meal she had

eaten and drunk the night before. Usually, she emptied out
the pail in the toilet in the early mornings before I even
climbed out of bed. I couldn't say why I was so annoyed at
being greeted with her bowel movements. At first, I thought
it was her negligence that upset me, but then I realized, plain
and simple, that I was angry that she had left the pail and
created the opportunity to disgust me. At the time, I didn't
understand why my grandmother was so angry when she
came home to meet my annoyance and scorn. It was the
complaint I greeted her with when she walked into the house.
She wanted to know what I was doing in her bedroom, and
if the pail bothered me, why hadn't I emptied it myself. She
wanted to know why I left the pail in her bedroom for the
entire day for her to come home and throw it out. She wanted
to know how I could scorn the woman who had cleaned my
vomit and wiped my behind and changed the sheets when I
used to wet the bed. The whole incident bothered and embarrassed me, and my grandmother was so angry that she left
me to prepare my own dinner. I hadn't gone into her bedroom since.

"Wah yuh doin' down 'ere?" my grandmother wanted to
know down at Mermaid River. I remember she was looking
over me carefully, and using her hand to shade her eyes,
which made the bangs on her wig scrunch up. She braided
her hair in little plaits but I only saw them early in the mornings or late at night because she wore a wig everywhere. "Oh,
I just come down to help you." This made my grandmother
look at me hard, as though I was telling her stories.

As suspicious as she appeared, she also looked happy to

see me. She could show me off to Mrs. Angie and Mrs. Wright, explaining how I always brought home the highest marks in school. She offered me the piece of foil she was eating from. It was a piece of jerk chicken, still warm as I used my fingers to break the flesh apart. Mrs. Angie was roasting jerk chicken in a steel drum and Mrs. Wright was roasting yams, saltfish, and corn in another one. They were across the road from Mermaid River, under a tree where everything they needed was laid out: chairs for sitting, an umbrella, paper fans, and a Bible and church hymnal and other necessities I can't remember. The tree was in front of the house where Mrs. Angie lived with her husband. On one of the two front walls of the house were painted the words WE SELL HOT GOOD FOOD, big enough for the people in passing vehicles to make out. Every morning my grandmother woke up early to prepare various sweets, like tamarind balls, coconut drops, and plantain tarts. Then she walked down to Mermaid River to sit under that tree with her two friends. On the days it rained, if the rain was very bad, they all stayed home. But if it was only a drizzle, Mrs. Angie would get her husband to tie a piece of tarpaulin under the tree.

There are three black students in my chemistry class. And then there is me. When I told my mother this, she said I shouldn't worry with those things. The *and then there is me* part was supposed to be funny but she didn't get it. My mother wants to keep me strong to make sure I do something important with my life. My stepfather is a garbage collector, which must have been a disappointment to my mother. Once, I heard her tell her friend that she never wanted to marry a man who came home with dirt under his fingernails. The irony of my mother marrying a garbage collector, the exact kind of man she didn't want to marry, filled the next moments with laughter. I could hear my mother's friend laughing on the other end of the phone. But my mother says my stepfather's job is very good money in this country, and nothing to be ashamed of, and she says this to convince the both of us, and to meet our surprise, because where we come from nobody with any shame would willingly collect people's garbage for a living.

When class ends, I walk up to the chemistry teacher to show him the letter. He is an old white man with thinning hair, who smells of cigarettes and something else we can't put our fingers on. He is known to make at least one student a semester, usually a girl, openly cry. He is also known as the only teacher who cusses in class, saying, for example, "I don't give a rat's ass" whenever someone gives him an excuse. Now he says to me, "I'm sorry for your loss." This is a surprise to hear from him, but how he says it feels appropriate since it's the uncaring way he always speaks. He must have lived a hard life—that's what my mother says about people who are miserable. And then he says it's okay that I'm going to Jamaica, but make sure I get the notes from someone when I get back. I thank him and leave the classroom.

I show the letter to all my teachers. Mrs. Cunningham, my French teacher, looks very sorry for me because this is the kind of person she is. She looks like she is about to hug me but she remembers herself so she only puts her hand on my shoulder. My classmates want to know what's in the letter because they are nosy. I see them looking at me.

The day I went down to help her, my grandmother and I sat under the tree, waiting for customers. She started telling me about old times—how the river used to be fat, how it used to be unnamed. Eventually a tour bus pulled up across the road, everyone disembarked, and we watched a tour guide talk to a group of people. Then the tourists were taking photos and a few crossed the road and bought jerk chicken, roasted corn, saltfish, and yams. One woman bought a dozen coconut drops from my grandmother, explaining that she was taking them back home with her. As afternoon pushed into evening, cars pulled up alongside the tree. Mrs. Angie and Mrs. Wright would get up to take the orders. I collected one of everything my grandmother prepared and held them out by the top of the plastic bags she tied them in, so customers could see what we had for sale.

By the time the second tour bus pulled up to Mermaid River, I had learned that as little girls my grandmother and her friends from primary school tied up their uniform skirts to wade in the river. One time, they got it into their heads to wade in their drawers, so that's how they were, all four of them, and then they wrung out their drawers and hid them in their schoolbags and walked home holding down their uniform skirts in case a heavy wind blew.

Sometimes someone would go home with a busted-open

foot, a sharp stone having made its mark. The time it happened for my grandmother she was walking softly on that foot when her mother asked her, "Wah wrong wid yuh foot, gal?" "Nothing, ma'am," my grandmother said, and then she tried to walk normally on the foot, just until her mother shifted her attention to something else. Later my grandmother was made to reveal the foot, to lift it onto her mother's lap, because her mother once again noticed how lightly the foot was touching the ground. Somehow my great-grandmother knew the cut was from a stone in the river, so even while holding my grandmother's foot on her lap, she smacked the side of her daughter's head, hard enough for tears, because she wasn't allowed at the river without somebody grown watching. Later, though, my great-grandmother would find a piece of aloe vera to rub on the cut. And that day under the tree, the memory of the whole incident made my grandmother smile.

My closest friend is a Chinese boy named Jason. His real name is something else. Every time we have a new class, the teacher will try to pronounce his Chinese name and Jason will say, "Just call me Jason." We met freshman year in literature class because we sat next to each other, so we were always assigned to work together. When Jason asked where I was from and I said Jamaica, he complimented my English and asked what language Jamaicans speak. I laughed. That question is what I remember when I think about us first becoming friends.

We are the same: quiet, loyal, but mostly our commitment is because we were each other's first friend in a new school. Sometimes we forget each other. Jason will hang out with some other Chinese boys, and I will hang out with the smaller amount of black boys in our school. The black boys like me, especially because sometimes what I say that isn't meant to be funny is funny because I say it. Since I don't want to bother with the pizza they are serving in the cafeteria, and I see Jason with some other Chinese boys eating pizza, I go to the gym to watch the basketball game.

Before I moved to Brooklyn, I'd never played basketball before. We played cricket and football at my primary school. Since the game has already started, I sit on the bleachers and watch. Nicolas looks up and asks if I want to play. "Next game," I say, knowing that by the time the next game starts it will be time to head back to class. I like that they want to include me and I've grown to enjoy watching them play when I have nothing better to do, but as often as I can I try to get out of playing because I know I'm no good.

If I could play basketball better or had more interest in watching games with my stepfather, we would get along better. We get on fine. Nothing is wrong. I just know I am not the son he was hoping for. Sometimes my stepfather will see me studying and he says, "I could have used a little bit of that when I was your age," but I know he is also saying, "You are not how I was expecting." Sometimes I'll sit for a while to watch a game with him and I can tell my presence pleases him. When he and my mother picked me up from the airport, he touched my shoulder and smiled; later he would laugh at my accent. My mother told me that because he is older than she is, he didn't want to bother with any babies, which is why he was glad to hear that she already had a son. They married just before they sent for me, since my mother didn't want me to think of her without respect. She said she couldn't bring me into any living arrangement with a man she wasn't married to. She is always telling me everything, even what she is ashamed for me to know. This is how my mother kneads the eight years away.

Sometimes I want to lie on my bed in the middle of the day, which is another thing my stepfather doesn't understand about me. I just lie there thinking, with my hands folded under my head, and sometimes I fall asleep. When I lived with my grandmother, I used to sit up in the mango tree to think or when I had to memorize something for school. One time, my grandmother told me that the man next door complained that I was sitting in the mango tree because I wanted to peep on him. But when my grandmother told me this, she was smiling when she really wanted to be laughing at the man. Because she did things the old way, she didn't want to laugh at him in front of me because she didn't want me to forget I was a child. I smiled back at her, because this old man was known to be miserable and forever convinced that people were stealing from him, or watching him, or talking his business.

All those years later, my grandmother still went back to Mermaid River, though she hadn't let the water touch her in years. She faced her history even while she made her future. All her life, she only called one place home, and she watched it build up and change so that some parts didn't bear any resemblance. As a little girl walking to and from school, she'd become familiar with the modest stretch of concrete and zinc houses whose backyards dipped into the river. In the afternoons, a woman used to sit on one of the verandas discreetly breastfeeding a fat baby. Next door lived a couple that seemed to enjoy cursing each other at their gate. A cherry tree leaned out of one of the yards, which attracted schoolchildren. When the houses and the inhabitants were gone, the government finally looked about the potholes in the roads. My grandmother packed her basket every morning and walked the twenty minutes to the river where people will remember her, if they remember her, as an old woman selling from a basket when they got off the bus. Or stopped their car to see Mermaid River, maybe to take a photograph by the sign. Perhaps they heard the story given by the tour guide, or read it in a pamphlet, or they knew it for themselves. An old-time story about how old-time people used to see a mermaid combing her hair on the bank of the river. The mermaid is said to have jumped back into the water when she realized she was being watched. WELCOME TO MERMAID RIVER and in smaller print, "No swimming, the rocks are sharp." Always, someone will dip his or her foot into the water, since the sign only forbids swimming.

Only now does the history of that river sit on me. I realize that my grandmother had a world all her own, one that excluded me because I'd never thought of her as a little girl or as anyone other than the woman who took care of me until the real woman who should have been taking care of me was set up good enough to send for me.

The day after I helped my grandmother down at Mermaid River, I still had the fire lit under me, so I flung the coconuts against the cement at the back of the house. I cracked open tamarinds and, following my grandmother's instructions, folded them into little balls with sugar. I got to school a few minutes early and was shocked to see Roger Boxx playing cricket. That was how he would level out his height; he turned out to be the strongest cricket player in our school. And he brought me along. He convinced the other boys to look past my overall mediocrity and my subpar batting skills, and then my mornings and afternoons were filled with cricket. The first few days, I felt guilty because of the thought of my grandmother, an old woman, who I should have been helping. But guilt often loses its flavor, I've found. My grandmother shook her head when I raced out of the house in the mornings. She said she should have known it was too good to be true, but I knew she missed me. The morning I started leaving early again, I left the coconuts on the dining table. I left them even though I knew they were laid out for me to crack.

I close my eyes on the plane. I see three old women under a tree laughing a dancing laugh. My mind doesn't recognize who they are and still I want to tell one of them, "I never seen you laugh like that but once the whole time I knew you."

I open my eyes and I can't say whether I was dreaming or re-membering, maybe both.

My cricket days ended when the school year came to a close because my mother finally sent for me. She had mar-ried a man for love. It also solved the problem of getting her papers. Now I am back, finally, for my grandmother's funeral. In the city, the heat feels as if it wants to knock us down; that's what my mother says, she says the heat wants to knock us down. I have been craving the sunshine the whole time I've been away. On our way from the airport, my mother convinces the taxi man to stop in the city. All because my stepfather wants oxtail from a restaurant he ate from when he visited the island with another woman long before he knew my mother. My stepfather says he has been thinking of the oxtail for the past seven years. I see my mother look at him because she cooks oxtail in New York whenever he wants it. I see the look she gives him and I understand be-cause I am her child. The look passes, and then my mother is telling my stepfather to buy enough oxtail for all of us.

This is how my mother and I are alone in Kingston, Ja-maica, such a small place on the globe in my World History class that if you aren't careful you can easily miss it. At the market, there are so many people, most of them trying to sell us something. There is a man selling string crafts, he has them stacked up top of his head and he is shouting that the crafts are patterned into the hummingbird, the national bird. There is a woman selling bammy from a basket on her head. There are fruit stands and men roasting meat, corn, and yams. My mother's head is turning to look at everything and everyone because she so badly wants to use the spending money she budgeted.

Long after my mother and I have eaten, my stepfather is still sucking the oxtail bones.

The taxi is driving my mother, my stepfather, and me to my grandmother's house, where we will meet relatives before the funeral tomorrow. Even though I'm waiting to see Mermaid River, I almost miss it. Because on the other side of the street, there is a tree and behind the tree is a blue house that used to be painted yellow. There is no longer a sign that reads, WE SELL HOT GOOD FOOD. There are no old women laughing a dancing laugh.

I can't remember this, but my grandmother used to say I would sleep on her breast after my mother left. I cried when she put me in bed by myself, so she put me in bed next to her. She said I used to fall asleep with my head on one of her breasts. This embarrassed me because it was a story that my grandmother repeated often to her friends and I realized early that old women breasts were something I should stay far away from. I didn't know what about the story pleased her to retell it. Now I think maybe she was trying to say, "Listen, to how this boy loves me."

THE GHOST OF JIA YI

FOR SHAO TONG

Tiffany can't sleep when she hears that police found Jia Yi, the missing international student, dead in the trunk of her car. The news anchor reported that "a person of interest," the man Jia Yi had been spending time with, had already flown back to China, and that someone had stuffed her body in the trunk of her car as though she was less than a person. When Tiffany finally falls asleep in the early hours of the morning, she dreams that Jia whispers her killer's name in her ears. And isn't this what Tiffany's mother prayed against? She worried that she would lose her daughter tragically in America, a place that, according to the television and newspapers, took daughters and later spit out their bones. Tiffany had ignored her mother, even laughed at her because she believed her mother to be too country, too afraid of the world. But if it happened to someone else's daughter, who's to say that it couldn't happen to her?

Your first time to America, Iowa isn't where you expect to end up. Midwestern towns are at times charming, and stretches of farmland have been thought to be beautiful, but Iowa isn't the kind of place Jamaicans talk about when they talk about America. Before Tiffany left home, whenever she told people that she was moving to Iowa because a school offered her a track scholarship, they screwed up their faces because they'd only heard of the well-known places in the States. So she started to tell people that she was going to a place near Chicago, because Chicago might have been a place they'd heard of before. Sometimes, when things were really bad, she said, "Near where Oprah used to live."

Tiffany started running for the reasons all children run: the ground fleshy under her feet, a day thick with possibility, and how else to keep up? And then she discovered running a second time because it was a way to beat and impress her brother. When they were children, Kareem's favorite game was to tease his sister, like calling her Coconut Head because her hair was short. Whenever he played in the yard with the boys who lived next door, he refused to include Tiffany. She sat on the front steps watching them play football or marbles, and sometimes she was bold enough to ask them if she could join them. While the other boys wouldn't have minded, her brother always told her no. She didn't understand why he disliked her so much. It wasn't until she was older that she could look back to see that he resented her for taking up all the attention when she was born premature. Their parents were so relieved that she lived that their gratitude looked like favoritism.

At first, when Tiffany realized that she couldn't gain the affection of her brother, she carried her complaints to her parents, who made Kareem play with her. But this never really worked; it just made her brother resent her even more. So she started fighting him. When he called her Coconut Head, she called him Fat Head. And when he looked at her as though he would have stepped on her if she was a cockroach, she laughed in his face. But underneath her laughter, she still yearned for her brother's love.

Early one evening, Tiffany's mother sent her to call Kareem from the schoolyard where he was playing with his friends, because it was almost dinnertime. The school was a short distance from their house, so she ran all the way there. Those days, if Tiffany could run somewhere, even when it was preferable that she walked because she was, for example, wearing church shoes, she ran. That day, once she got to the back of the school, a large grassy area where students took recess, she expected Kareem and his friends to be playing cricket, but instead she saw that they were about to race. Their bodies were bent in the starting position she'd seen people on the television take. One of her brother's friends was a distance away from the rest, so she assumed that he was the person who would say, "On your mark, set, go!" As she walked across to where her brother and his friends were crouched, they started running, and without thinking about it, she joined the race. When she beat all of them, Kareem and his friends looked at her as though although they'd known her for a long time, they'd only just thought to really look at her. One of them asked Kareem, "Mek yuh neva tell me seh yuh likkle sistah can run?" After that, Kareem often called upon Tiffany to race his friends and classmates in order to prove that he wasn't lying when he said that his little sister could beat anybody.

When Tiffany wakes up, the ghost of Jia Yi is on the front and the back of her mind because while she slept, the ghost had drawn near to whisper in her ear, so close that Tiffany could have touched her. She wakes early to the winter sun streaming through the window, and to her roommate's loud snoring, always a surprise considering the girl's petite frame. Sometime during the night, Tiffany became overheated, and her comforter is lying on the ground. She lifts it onto the bed, enclosing her body in a darker cave of morning, willing herself to fall back asleep to see if Jia Yi comes again to whisper her killer's name. The name had felt on the tip of Tiffany's tongue because it had been one of those dreams that touched the living world.

Jia does come back, though this time they are sitting across from each other in one of the Chinese restaurants in town. Jia is eating a dish that looks more traditional than the chicken and broccoli in front of Tiffany, which means that she must have ordered from the traditional menu. Jia is eating quickly, sometimes pausing to look at her phone, and she isn't paying any mind to Tiffany. It isn't until she picks up her bag and brings her tray to the garbage bin that Tiffany realizes that she was mistaken in thinking that they were eating together when in fact they were strangers sitting across from each other in a restaurant crowded during lunch hour. Jia's hair is long and black, hanging to the middle of her back. Before she leaves the restaurant, she looks behind her in the direction of where she had been sitting, presumably to see if she left anything behind. Looking at her face, Tiffany remembers that the news anchor said that she was twenty, but she could have passed for sixteen.

Tiffany's roommate, Taylor, is shaking her awake, asking if she plans to miss the 8 a.m. class they have together. Tiffany considers this: the Introduction to Psychology class allows one absence, which she hasn't used as yet. "I'm tired," she lies. "Take notes for me?" Taylor agrees easily, her heavily lined eyes appraising Tiffany because she's never skipped class before. Taylor is a white girl from a small town in Iowa, and Tiffany suspects that besides Taylor's boyfriend, she is the only other black person she's had close contact with, and definitely the first foreigner she's known with any kind of intimacy. Taylor is kind but annoying. She would take off her Victoria's Secret sweatpants with the word PINK on her ass to lend to Tiffany, but she's chattier than Tiffany would prefer in a roommate. She teases Tiffany that she is a Jamaican who won't smoke marijuana with her, and who won't let her smoke in their dorm room. "I didn't come to America to smoke ganja," Tiffany says, even though she knows that Taylor won't understand what she means. She doesn't add that she's never smoked weed, because she knows that Taylor is stupid enough to be shocked by this fact.

Taylor gets her weed from her boyfriend, Kevin, a tall black guy from Chicago, who Tiffany thinks looks too sleepy-eyed to be a biochem major. Mostly he ignores Tiffany and she ignores him, when she isn't looking at him through the corner of her eyes. She's decided that he's almost handsome from the right angle. White men on campus look through and around her, so it hurt her to meet this black man who behaved as though she wasn't anyone to get to know. This is how come Tiffany was surprised when, as usual, she came into the room to see that Taylor had gone to class and left Kevin on her computer, and when she grunted hello and closed the door, he was behind her, then he was pushing her against the door, and looking down at her as though it wasn't anything, as though he didn't have a girlfriend and Tiffany wasn't his girlfriend's roommate, and soon they were naked and tangled in her bed, and it was hot, and she had thought: *So this is what they call fucking.* She'd only ever been with one other man, and sex with him had been an affectionate, cautious introduction. Taylor came back to see that Kevin was still using her computer and Tiffany was taking a shower. Later, Tiffany was surprised to remember that it had been she who initiated things, reaching up to kiss Kevin, wrapping her legs around him.

She lies in bed now, listening to Taylor bustle around the

room, then go into the bathroom, emerging out of it with glossy lips, reentering and then reemerging with her hair pulled into a ponytail. Tiffany realizes that the dream of the restaurant had felt as sharp as a memory. And couldn't it have happened? Couldn't she have sat across from Jia Yi and it wouldn't have meant a thing? Tiffany would have barely looked at her, registering her as another Asian student on campus, forgettable, invisible, not like how she would have taken her in had she been a black girl she didn't know and she'd maybe even have spoken to her. America, the land of diversity, where people talk to who they think it's safest to talk to.

As soon as Taylor leaves, pulling the door shut behind her, Tiffany buries herself again under the comforter. But sleep won't come to her. Jia Yi won't come back.

Tiffany was sure that God made her to run. Running made her feel as though the world carried her on its wings. Whenever she suffered some social atrocity, like the time the boys in her class made a list of the prettiest girls and hadn't included her, she reminded herself that someday when she won a gold medal at the Olympics, Jamaicans would dance in the streets. So what if her first boyfriend left her for another girl? He returned to his ex-girlfriend even though he had held her hand and promised that the loss of her virginity to him would be a safe thing. So what if her father's affair led to an outside child and the dissolution of her parents' marriage? She could not look at either of her parents without feeling sorry for them. But she had running and it belonged only to her.

She never imagined that she wouldn't be good enough. Four years in a row, she tried out for the island-wide youth competition, the same competition that the Olympians she admired had raced and won. Every year, she had come last in her category, girls ages 14–18, tears running down her face when she crossed the finish line. People said she had potential. Two trainers offered to work with her to see how she would improve. She asked herself: *What is the point if I'm not the best?* It wasn't that she was cocky, but it was a purer feeling. What she'd felt for all those years, how far she believed that her running would take her, is what people call faith.

Later, when the recruiters from American universities came to Jamaica, her mother pushed her to try out. Tiffany wasn't surprised to hear that she was good enough for an athletic scholarship. And her family, especially her mother, had been so thrilled that running could take her so far, that it seemed her only option was to smile as though she too was proud.

Midday Tiffany wakes from a different dream. She had been leading in a race against Kevin, Taylor, and Jia Yi, but at the finish line her teeth started to fall from her mouth. She leaves the dormitory for a frappe at one of the coffee shops downtown. Wearing her team sweatshirt, which is almost too warm for the sunny mid-March day, she jogs past students walking to and from classes. She figures that sugar, that cure-all, will calm her nerves. In the last few months, she's become addicted to frappes because Taylor works as a barista and occasionally brings drinks home. Tiffany is looking into the window of the Taiwanese tea shop when Duane taps her on the shoulder, which causes her to flinch dramatically.

"Everything all right with you?" He looks her over carefully. She'd felt someone come up behind her. But she hadn't seen anyone. She'd only felt the person bump into her, and then for some reason she was certain the person had entered the tea shop though she had no reason for thinking so. But she can't tell Duane any of this, can she?

"Do you believe in ghosts?" she asks.

"Ghosts? Why are you asking me about ghosts?"

"I had a weird experience at home, and just now someone I didn't see bumped my shoulder."

He laughs. "Tiffany, yuh no memba when mi say you fi be'ave yuhself?" He's referring to a recent time when he saw her and her fellow underage teammates downing shots at a bar downtown.

"Mi nah play! Yuh believe in duppy?"

"My professor was saying that most of the universe is dark matter, which means that we really don't know what's out there," he says, talking in his serious way that is adorable to Tiffany. "So if yuh saying that yuh being haunted by a duppy, it no matter wah mi believe."

"It's Jia Yi."

"Di Chinese girl dem find dead?! You knew her? I had a class with her."

"You had a class wid her? What was she like? Mi neva know her."

"She was nice. One time we ha' fi work together. She laughed nuff. She didn't like *Invisible Man*. Are you sure that the situation nah mess wid your head? Maybe the fact that everyone a talk 'bout her?" He was watching her carefully. He was the only person who knew about the pills the psychiatrist prescribed.

"Dat must be what's happening."

"Yuh sound doubtful. Listen, mi ha' fi run. Let's touch base later."

Tiffany turns to watch him go. His mother, who is of Chinese ancestry, runs a small grocery store back home with his father, a black man. People on campus never believe that he's Jamaican. Before she started hooking up with Kevin, they almost hung out romantically. Duane would cook curry chicken, they'd watch a movie, and inevitably the night would end with kissing. He'd been recruited to run too, but he had no passion for it, which Tiffany envied. It was merely a means to what he wanted and it had worked, as he was off to medical school in Cuba in the fall. There was a girl back home he wanted to marry when he was old enough. He felt that too many Jamaicans were quick to forget their country, relocating to foreign economies. He wanted to earn his degrees and return home.

The last time Tiffany spoke to her mother, she lied and told her that the team won their most recent meet. She also told her mother that she has decided to become a nurse, because this seems like an honorable enough profession, but really she can't think of anything else to become. Before Tiffany decided on a major, her mother would say some variation of, "Tiffany, I know yuh wan' fi run but yuh cyaan guarantee dat." To quickly steer the conversation elsewhere, so she wouldn't be drawn into lying any more than she had to, Tiffany would tell stories about Taylor's family. Her mother likes to hear stories about white people almost as much as Taylor likes to share them. There is the fact that Taylor's sister and her husband are getting divorced because her sister was having an affair with a woman. There is also the fact that Taylor discovered a sex toy in her mother's chest of drawers, which surprised her because her father is such a conservative man. Tiffany's mother would ask some variation of, "Mi wonder if all white people mek it a habit fi chat dem family business like dat?" Tiffany described the coffee shop where Taylor was a barista—by opening time at 5:30 a.m., people started to line up at the door. "Coo yah!" her mother said, surprised to learn about the caffeinated destiny of that treasured Blue Mountain coffee that Jamaica exported. Tiffany also described the cold weather she could barely manage, but how the snow made everything quiet, like Sunday mornings.

But there is plenty Tiffany doesn't tell her mother. She doesn't tell her mother about her first few months here, when running couldn't save her, when it couldn't do a thing for her. The cold weather depressed her, the dark mornings kept her spirits low, and she craved a fulfilling plate of food. One restaurant in town served what the menu called a "jerk burger," and Tiffany had been so excited by the idea of Jamaican food that she hadn't considered that the menu's definition of jerk could be a beef patty that came covered in jerk sauce and mango salsa. She was so disappointed she almost wanted to cry. She missed Champion, her overfed dog, who licked her feet when she sat on the veranda. And she missed sitting on the veranda, where she loved to idle, sometimes clipping and filing her nails, other times reading one of the romance books a friend loaned her, and she would call out to neighbors as they walked past. The daughter of two secondary school teachers, she had been raised on middle-class pride in a house her parents built from the ground up. But that upbringing where she was raised neither poor nor rich was no more, now that her father lived with the other woman, her brother had moved to another parish, and her mother rented out the bedrooms so that she wouldn't have to live alone.

In America, Tiffany yearns for someone who understands her. Duane tries, but inevitably they misunderstand each other. He doesn't understand why she isn't happier at the chance of an American education, and she doesn't understand how he's assimilated so quickly to American life. He has a friend, Jamal from Philadelphia, the other black guy on the team, who translates things for him. Once, Tiffany heard Duane say to Jamal, "Tell me about African Americans." Most of the other girls on the track and field team are white, plenty of them Iowan or from places that to Tiffany might as well be Iowa. There is another black girl, who had been recruited from Kenya, but she wants to forget where she came from. She pays Tiffany little attention, preferring to hang out with the white girls, and speaks as though she is trying to strip Nairobi from her voice.

Tiffany would have stopped going to practice if it didn't mean that she would lose her scholarship, and she knew that she would be ashamed to return to Jamaica empty-handed. But her lack of interest showed, and the coach reprimanded her. He advised her to see a counselor and warned how easy it was to lose an athletic scholarship and be sent home. He was a man with a warm, open face and a receding hairline, and at first he had seemed like an ally, but sitting in his office, Tiffany believed that he was serious about sending her home. When she went crying to Duane, he let her on to the unspoken expectation that international athletes were supposed to carry the team—to train harder, to run and jump farther. Later, when Tiffany saw the school psychologist, she was referred to a psychiatrist, who wrote a prescription for pills that helped with the daily task of living.

Tiffany was sure that she was meant to be famous. She was sure that the time would come when Jamaicans would memorize her first and last name when they watched her on their televisions representing Jamaica at the Olympics. Instead, she is in the middle of a country that isn't home to her, a country where women like her are more memorable dead than alive. That's the only way she'll end up on anyone's television. Her body would be flown back home and her mother, who believes that America is where young girls come to die, would be quick to tell everyone that this is exactly what she expected to happen, all her fears realized.

• • •

Once, Tiffany and Kevin went on a date together. It was at the beginning of the semester in late January, when they'd first started sleeping together. Taylor was with family for the weekend, so they'd driven thirty minutes in a car Kevin borrowed from a friend to a bigger city, where they were to meet up with his cousin, Wayne, who was visiting his child. Kevin kept the radio turned up high, and at stoplights he'd rub Tiffany's thigh. They ate in a restaurant that served Chinese food on pizza crust. She was disappointed to discover that they had little to say to each other. He was quiet by nature, and she didn't know how to open him up. They talked about classes, their birth order, and the weather, before she had the right idea of what to say when they returned to the car.

"Why didn't you stay in Chicago for school?" she asked, buckling her seatbelt.

He looked at her. "That came out of nowhere. Why didn't you stay in Jamaica?"

"Here they were offering to pay my tuition."

"Same with me. My mother said it was a waste not to come. But being around so many white people makes me nervous."

"What about Taylor?"

"What about her?"

"She's white."

He laughed. "So I've observed."

He put the key in the ignition and they rode silently for a while. Tiffany wanted to discuss the nature of their relationship, but she didn't know what to say. She thought it was sloppy how he pursued her in the very same room she shared with Taylor. It was almost as though he wanted to get caught. They were driving through the downtown area. It was larger and more energetic than where they went to school. She'd been told that it was the capital of Iowa.

"Before I came to America, I'd never heard of Iowa," she said.

"You heard of Chicago, though, right?"

"Yeah, Oprah used to live there, and that rapper who said that the president didn't care about black people."

"You mean Kanye." He laughed. "That was a long time ago. Kanye doesn't care about black people anymore."

Wayne was waiting for them in front of an exhausted-looking apartment complex. He was a short, wide man in his late twenties wearing a T-shirt with Biggie's face on it. In fact, he looked like Biggie himself. "What happened to the white girl?" he asked, stooping to look into the car. Kevin laughed a response. He and Wayne went into the house together. A little while later, Kevin returned, smelling of marijuana. He asked Tiffany if she wanted to come inside.

The apartment was the very definition of disorder. The center table was covered with empty food cartons, a pee-soaked diaper, various body care and makeup tubes, a few packages of condoms, and a bowl of soggy cereal. A beautiful white woman sat on the couch holding a sleeping toddler, whose brown face was caked in something he had eaten. When Tiffany sat next to her, she responded with a soft, vacant "Hi," before returning to her phone.

Across from them, Kevin and Wayne were sitting at the dining table having a heated conversation about a cousin, who was marrying a man they disliked. Twenty, then thirty minutes passed. Tiffany wanted to use the bathroom, but she was afraid of what would meet her there. The beautiful white woman left the sleeping child on the couch, picked up her purse and jacket, and slammed the front door behind her. She was wearing red leather pants, which made Tiffany think that she had someplace to be. Kevin and Wayne looked momentarily surprised, but then continued talking. "He called me a self-hating black man because my baby mother is white," Wayne was saying. "I told him, how you mean? Pussy is pussy." Kevin laughed. Wayne continued, "He said that black people in the Midwest fuck with hick-minded white people. I said to Britney, where you find this high and mighty nigga at? The club, she said." He and Kevin laughed. Tiffany stood. Wayne turned toward her. "My cousin says you run," he said.

"Yes," she said, waiting for whatever came next.

"What's your nationality?" he said, studying her carefully.

"She's Jamaican," Kevin said brightly, as though it was something he was proud of.

"Wha' gwan," Wayne said, laughing, but no one else joined him. He became serious. "Why are Jamaicans so fast?"

"Because it's a small island," Kevin said.

Wayne looked to him. "What does that have to do with anything?"

"It's a limited gene pool."

"Interesting. I hadn't thought of that." He turned back to Tiffany. "What do you think? What's your name again?"

"I wish I knew," she said. She was annoyed, but she didn't know why. "Where is the bathroom?"

Behind her, she could hear Wayne asking, "Did I say something to offend your girl?"

Later that night, when Tiffany and Kevin returned to campus, at the desolate corner where they would part ways, she asked, "What do you and Taylor talk about?" She'd observed that they mostly lay in bed watching Netflix. Apparently, they both loved to laugh. Kevin looked at her for a long moment. He was surprised. Perhaps, she would later consider, right then he was deciding never to ask her out again. Perhaps he was thinking that if he only slept with her, it would be easier for everyone involved. "Everything," he said, but he seemed unsure.

The news anchor said that the man identified as Jia Yi's boyfriend confided to a friend that he was displeased because she was seeing other men. It made Tiffany wonder what if it had been her in that trunk. Everyone would know that she had carried on with another woman's man. People would hear about her and believe that murder was the kind of thing to happen to a promiscuous girl. This is what Tiffany is thinking as Kevin pulls off her panties.

They don't talk. Kevin grunts, she moans, and sometimes he says dirty things to her. He looks at her lustfully, and though she is flattered, she knows that to him she is just a piece of ass. Still, he could be possessive. In the beginning he'd asked if she was sleeping with anyone else, and when she said that she wasn't, he'd nodded appreciatively. When he found out through the black student grapevine that she'd been hanging out with Duane, he texted her, "My friend says that you're a ho. Is that true?" She got upset, he apologized—claiming that he had been drinking—but it was obvious that for him their relationship didn't have room for anyone else.

During sex, Tiffany tries not to make extended eye contact, because something deep and disastrous is forming for him for these moments when his hands are on her breasts and then on her ass and then on her breasts again, and she's wondering if he smiles like this when he's with Taylor, if his hands are as busy for a white girl with small breasts and an ass that barely separates from her back.

Taylor's father hadn't been pleased to hear that she was dating a black man. When Kevin heard about it, he broke up with her first, but later they reconciled. As far as her father knows, she'd broken up with him the previous semester. But Tiffany sees Kevin holding Taylor's hand on campus, which means that in this threesome of a relationship, she's the biggest fool. Tiffany doesn't want to believe this, so she shakes her head because she doesn't want to be a fool, shakes her head because this is already complicated enough without adding feelings to the equation, shakes her head because she isn't the kind of girl to be along with another girl's man. But Kevin mistakes it as a symptom of the sex being good, so he grabs her hair to keep her steady, and she reaches for his other hand, holding it gently, lovingly. She isn't the first and she won't be the last woman to baptize her sorrows into the arms of a man. When she is with Kevin, it's easy to forget that America is a lonely place.

Tiffany's about to climax—any moment now—when the ghost of Jia Yi looks through her window. Tiffany screams and sits up abruptly, pushing Kevin off of her. He looks around, terrified, certain that Taylor has walked into the room. When he sees that his girlfriend isn't there, he says, "What is it?!" But Tiffany doesn't look at him. She's looking through the window to confirm that there isn't a tree or a fire escape or any other way for someone to climb to the third floor. After the tea shop, Jia Yi stayed away for three days, which gave Tiffany the opportunity to rationalize the haunting as evidence of her imagination. Now, she is quickly picking her clothes off the floor and dressing, and then she picks up Kevin's clothes and throws them at him. He looks at her with the slow realization that this thing they have is over. He asks the question of a man humbled by disappointment, "What happened?" But Tiffany doesn't answer him. How can she explain that her sins had been reflected on the face of a dead girl? She goes into the bathroom, where she peels off her clothes once again and takes a shower, soaping her body and rinsing, and repeating this process twice more, all the while crying and wondering if she is going crazy.

She isn't even sure that she believes in ghosts. When she was a child, Miss Palmer—the woman next door, who her mother fell out with—died before they could make up. Tiffany overheard her mother telling her father that some funny things had been happening in the house. Her mother said that several times while she had been cooking pork, she turned around for a moment and somehow the fire under the pots had been put out. Miss Palmer had believed that eating pork was sinful. Another time when her mother was taking a midday nap, she felt someone push their hand through the open window to put their hand on her head, combing their fingers through her hair. She jumped out of her sleep and looked out the window but there was no one there. Miss Palmer had been notorious for putting her hand in people's hair. Later, Tiffany's mother would have the church pastor visit to pray over the house, and after that, she never brought up Miss Palmer again.

A week later, Tiffany attends Jia Yi's memorial service. She's come directly from practice, so she's wearing sneakers and sweaty athletic clothes under her coat, but even if she had come in proper clothes, she would have still held back, standing a distance from the service, leaning against a tree. There are a little over two hundred people, most of them Asian, circled around a table with lit candles and a photograph of Jia Yi. The director of the International Studies Program is speaking, saying obvious things, the only things to say: Jia Yi was kind, intelligent, her death a loss because what a future and the things that could have been. When the candles are blown out and everyone is dispersing, Tiffany looks up at the sky, remembering a conversation she'd had with her father.

She'd gone home for winter break, and when she visited

her father, the woman he'd chosen over her mother was conveniently visiting her own mother with their love child. Tiffany and her father sat at the dining table eating the simple dinner of saltfish and green bananas he had prepared.

"So what yuh think, Tiffany? Jamaica too small fi yuh?" She laughed.

"You know, you and I always alike. We neva content. I remember when you was likkle and I went to Panama and brought back a doll for you. You looked at me and asked, 'Wha else?' " He laughed.

"Is that why you lef' Mommy? Because yuh neva content?"

"I respect your mother. She gave me two children. I met your mother when I was a young man."

There was a long pause.

"You know, I fret ova you," he said, and it was obvious that he was deliberately changing the subject.

"Fret over me why?"

"Yuh tek everything so serious. I don't want America fi swallow my one girl pickney. The other day I couldn't sleep. I was looking at the sky and thinking it's the same sky you see in Iowa. I prayed for you. Yuh know how long since mi pray?"

That night, Tiffany dreams that she catches a fish. In the dream, she is fishing in the river where her father taught her to swim, but then the river becomes the university's aquatic center. She stands on the bank of the pool holding the fish in her arms like it is a baby. Its face is almost human. Eventually, she returns it to the water.

Eventually, the ghost of Jia Yi stopped visiting Tiffany. Once, Tiffany saw her running on the treadmill at the gym, her long black hair flying behind her, and another time when Tiffany turned a corner in the library, Jia looked up from a table scattered with papers and textbooks, lifting a hot beverage from a local coffee shop to her lips. Slowly she disappeared from Tiffany's dreams, her reality, and never again did she whisper her killer's name.

Six months later, what happened to Jia Yi is still unresolved. If there is a heaven, perhaps it has a support group for women whose deaths don't have the dignity of closure for those who loved and knew them, and maybe this is where Jia Yi has gone. Only occasionally does Tiffany remember her. And when she does remember Jia Yi, it's with regret for all the times she failed to notice her.

HOW TO LOVE A JAMAICAN

The Israelites used to send a goat out into the wilderness, and leave the animal, the sins, there. The priest put his hands on the goat and spoke of all the ways the people wronged God, and then someone would lead the goat away. No animal was sacrificed, no person had to die, it all felt quiet to me, as if forgiveness could be peaceful. Earlier today, when I asked Jacinth if she thought forgiveness could be quiet like that, she shrugged over her cornmeal porridge. I ask questions that cause her to think too hard and sometimes she responds, but most times she shrugs. When we first met and during the early times of our marriage, before children, my questions used to charm her. She used to say, "Wally, you have a mind fah both ah we," because where her mind stopped short, mine roamed, barely ever quieting. One time she told me, "You ha fi tink 'bout everything." And then she asked me, "Dat don't tire you?"

When I was a little boy, my mother used to call me fast. "Wallace, why yuh ha fi fass inna people business?" There were many times I embarrassed her, asking Miss Brown why her children didn't have a father or asking Mr. Latchman why he didn't have any teeth in his mouth. My mind is like water—it flows into the deepest crevices. It wants to point a flashlight into dark corners. Asking, for example, if church people realize that the heaven they're selling sounds like a long church service, and, if they are right, who wants to listen to sermons forever? I wonder if there is a point where my talk ceased to impress Jacinth, or if it happened slowly over time.

The first time I spoke to Jacinth, I asked a question, though the simplest of questions. I had only been in New York for three months and I was lost in Manhattan. My mother's half brother was putting me up in Brooklyn, and he knew Joy, a woman from church, who cleaned and cooked for a wealthy family that was looking for a male caretaker for the elderly father who had recently moved in. I needed to be strong enough to help an elderly man into his wheelchair and into the shower, and willing to escort him to his doctor appointments or to see a movie or eat in a restaurant or wherever else he wanted to go. I was also to pretend to know Joy so well that the family would believe I was her nephew. When my uncle explained the situation, I remember I asked him,

"You see how church people lie?" I saw a young black woman pushing a stroller with a white baby in my direction. I stopped her for directions. She started laughing and asked me how long since I left Jamaica. I heard the island in her voice too— she told me that she hadn't left for a full year yet. Jacinth pushed the stroller all the way to the apartment building because she said she wasn't good at explaining directions. When I tell people how we met, Jacinth allows me to say that she wanted to look some more into my face and that's why she walked me to the building. She smiles and shakes her head and allows me to exaggerate. Before I entered the building, I took my pen out of my pocket and wrote her number in the palm of my hand.

Now Jacinth has come out of the house, where she is preparing our lunch. In New York, we alternate the cooking. By the time I met Jacinth, not even in New York for a year and she had learned enough about feminism to explain the kind of Jamaican woman she refused to be. But back on the island, we've fallen into Jamaican ways. Not purposefully, but because Jacinth hogs the kitchen. Cooking bloody meat from animals we can trace to the owners and vegetables we can dust the dirt from has instilled a new love for cooking in her. We are living in the house I was raised in, though it's a different house now. When I was growing up, there was an outside bathroom and half of the house lay unfinished. My father finished four rooms—two small bedrooms, a living room, a small inside kitchen—but the other half of the house, which was to be a dining room and another bedroom, lay unfinished for many years after he took up with another woman and moved to England with her. As a man, I sent money home for my mother to finish the house.

I am sitting on the tree stump clipping my toenails and I feel her eyes on me. I call the stump my "thinking seat." Jacinth calls it my "idle seat." I have become married to the stump—it's where I sit after meals while the food digests or when I want to do a little reading or writing, or sometimes I don't do anything at all. I just sit here and think—all kinds of thoughts and memories come to me. Yesterday, I remembered a dress my mother used to wear. A flowered dress and she is walking into the schoolyard to collect me. Where did that come from? And why? That's what I don't understand about memories. A little quiet and the mind will do its job, pulling all kinds of moments from the deepest caves for my remembering.

We cut down the pear tree because the fruit for some reason—Jacinth thought the roots were diseased—never ripened edible. The flesh was always brown and tasted off, and when the fruit fell in the backyard it created too much work to clean up. Not even the mongrel, a stray that plants himself daily outside our front door looking hungry, wanted to eat the pears. Jacinth picked two pears from the ground and put them on his plate next to the homemade dog food. She made cooked cornmeal with pieces of chicken. He ate the cornmeal, sniffed each pear, and started to sip water from his bowl. Jacinth and I laughed. We were watching because we both wanted to see if the dog would eat the pears.

"Since when dog don't eat pear?"

"What yuh saying? Even mongrel know good food. You tink dog a fool?"

The rotting pears on the ground behind the house bothered us. We didn't like when we accidentally stepped on one, because the rotting flesh not only dirtied the bottom of our shoes but it also smelled nasty. It seemed like a sin for all the pears to go to waste. Together we contemplated what a shame it was that we had to buy pears with a tree behind our house. We imagined that if the tree had been good to us we would eat pear for every meal, if the tree's bearing allowed for it: pear with fried dumplings for breakfast, pear with the pumpkin soup at lunchtime, pear alongside the rice and peas and stew chicken at dinnertime. Plus sometimes the fruits fell on the zinc roof of the chicken coop, scaring the chickens. Jacinth said the chickens wouldn't lay eggs if they were frightened, and I didn't believe her but she kept nagging me about the tree, so I finally cut it down. The chickens started laying more eggs and the stump is the best sitting spot in the yard.

Jacinth is still standing above me as I'm bent over my toes, both of us examining my nails that have grown thicker and yellow with age—my toenails and the little love handles around my waist remind me of my sixty-seven years. I have my mother's toenails now. I remember once when she and I were watching cricket in the living room during one of her last visits to New York and I looked down at her toes and it seemed as though I hadn't looked at her feet in twenty years. When had her toenails grown so ugly? The woman who raised me always had neat little toenails she sometimes kept painted. I couldn't reconcile that woman with the one who sat beside me, her toenails thick and yellow, unpleasant to look at.

I couldn't remember if I had cut my toenails in the last year and I wouldn't be bothered with the rusty nail clipper if it wasn't for what happened at the shop yesterday. I had been watching the domino game with Ugly, eating slices of watermelon Old Henry sold to us, when Old Henry's little granddaughter came out of the shop and started looking at my toenails. She couldn't be more than three years old. She stared at my toenails with such interest that she stooped down to get a closer look. I was surprised at the boldness of the child. The domino players and Ugly became interested too. They all watched quietly. We all started to laugh when one of her little fingers reached down to touch one of my toenails.

Jacinth is still watching me struggle with the rusty nail clipper. This morning she couldn't find the nail clipper she usually uses but she found an old one of my mother's. Yesterday, after Richie and the rest of them playing dominoes forgot about me, Ugly still chuckled softly beside me. "Bwoy," he said, "likkle pickney a di biggest bitch." As soon as I walked into the house, I asked Jacinth if she knew the whereabouts of a nail clipper. "A wah old man? Yuh see one hot young ting down di road that mek you wan fi groom yuhself?" I laughed heartily because she had stumbled so closely to the truth. And although she didn't understand why I laughed so loudly but because she enjoyed the pleasure of her joke hitting me so hard, Jacinth started to laugh too. She laughed even harder when I told her about the little girl. And for the rest of the evening, she would remember the image of the little girl bending to touch my toe and she would start laughing again.

I know Jacinth is here to ask me something but she's distracted watching me. Right before she opens her mouth to speak, I anticipate it. Maybe her breathing changes, or another change so subtle that another person wouldn't know to listen for it. That's how well I've memorized her after all these years. "Why you asking me about forgiveness for?" I look up at her because I am surprised that she has returned to the question. I expected to hear another kind of question. Maybe one related to the meal she is cooking. I am searching her face for answers, to see if she suspects the boy or that I have anything at all to hide from her, but I can't read that there is anything besides curiosity in her face. "No reason," I say. "I read something and was wondering." It's true. I had been reading my mother's old Bible. It's on the dresser by her bed, and sometimes I flip through it. My whole life it's the only book my mother kept beside her bed, and flipping through it, pausing to read a little bit, remembering how my mother used to say that when I left Jamaica I forgot God— and I used to argue back, in the calm, respectful way I was raised to talk to her, that I didn't forget God, I just didn't attend church—is calming, is refreshing in a way I couldn't begin to explain to someone. I shrug my shoulders to show Jacinth the conversation about forgiveness isn't a big thing at all, that I have forgotten it, so she should too. I continue clipping my toenails. Jacinth watches me for a moment, and then she is walking off to finish the lunch.

• • •

I watch her as she walks away from me, entering back into the house. She is wearing my favorite wig—usually she wears short wigs but this one is long to her shoulders, with bangs. It creates youthfulness about her face, reminding me of when we first met because she had a similar hairstyle. That day after she pushed the stroller to my destination, I accidentally washed her number off my hand. I didn't realize until I looked down at the smudged ink on my palm. I was disappointed. I didn't have plans to call, but I wanted the option to. Dropping my palm to my side, and surveying the faces on the train car, my eyes rested on her. My mouth stood open. New York seemed so much bigger in the early days, but I quickly learned better. She was laughing, later she would admit that she had been watching me for a few train stops already.

Recently, we went to town. We had walked through the market, and every way we turned, sellers were begging us to buy something from them. The market smelled of cooking meat, corn and yams roasting, the sweet, living smell of ripe fruits and vegetables mixed up with the smell of market men and women, sweat everywhere—under the arms, between the legs, on foreheads—and the perfumes and lotions of the customers coming to shop. All of these smells swirling, mixing with the smell of rotting food in the garbage dump. And if there was a smell for hardship, for hustling, for that feeling when someone leaves your sweet-sweet guineps to buy the little sour ones from so-and-so even after tasting yours, even after you lowered the price a little, it would smell like something that burns your nose and waters your eyes. If someone could bottle a smell for all the feelings in the market, it would be as sweet as the sweetest-smelling mango and as bad smelling as the market madman who walks around picking up fruit that rolled off somebody's heap.

Afterwards we went to buy jerk chicken from the men who cook the chicken in steel drums. Two of the four of them started motioning to us when they saw us walking toward them. When we approached them, another one of them had already shared out a piece of chicken wrapped in foil that he wanted to hand to me. He only wanted to hear if I wanted a larger serving. The whole thing was exhausting. When people warned us, "Watch dat people nuh smell foreign pon yuh," we didn't pay them any mind. We thought we knew how to dress, talk, and act like we belonged—and to us, we do belong. No amount of years living in America could convince us that this place isn't our home. One time my daughter showed me a photo she took when she had gone upstate to visit a friend. In the photo, the grass, the trees, the mountains were covered with snow and the word "beautiful" came to my mind. But that's uncommon for me. It's more natural that I'm the man arguing that God didn't mean for ice to fall from the sky. I'm the man arguing that God meant for summer day after day and that winter was the devil's idea.

We love to go to town to see all kind of people passing through. Mothers holding the hands of the children they just picked up from school. The day has worn on the children—they entered the classroom with shiny faces and neat hair, packaged so as not to shame their parents, but now the wrapping paper is frayed. Old women wearing old church shoes in town for the day, on their way to doctor appointments or to pick up medicine. Young men in street clothes, walking quickly as if they have somewhere to go, or idling around calling out to women or discussing this or that amongst themselves in front of Mr. Chang's shop. High school students in their uniforms: the girls from Bishop Gibson in their purple jumper dresses, white shirts white-white, hair neatly combed, while the boys wear khaki uniforms. Jamaican children wearing their school uniforms are as beautiful as flowers. That's what Jacinth said, and I nodded in agreement. When we sent our children to public school, it occurred to us how strange it was that so many American schools didn't require uniforms. We ached for our daughters, both of them never having to kneel over their white school shirts, scrubbing with blue bar soap until the fabric glistened white. A teacher would never pass our daughters in the halls and ask why they neglected to iron their uniforms or polish their shoes or comb their hair neatly or why they were wearing white socks since it was against the uniform policy. We stood under the shade of a building eating our jerk chicken and people-watching when a taxi man started beeping his horn at us. We didn't want to hear from anyone else looking to make money from us, and because we were preoccupied with eating, we ignored him. But the beeping continued, so I looked over to recognize a face I couldn't put a name to. After reintroductions were made—the man was a son of one of my mother's church friends—the man, Eddie, drove us home.

"But, Wally, yuh look like seh yuh still a young boy?"

We hadn't seen each other in over twenty-five years. Eddie reminded me that during a trip home, I had seen him at my mother's church and we shook hands after the service. He had aged, the years pulled youth from his face.

"Yes, and I'm his old lady," Jacinth said, and we all laughed.

But under my laughter I felt a sadness I couldn't name and I wondered if Jacinth felt it too. In preparatory school they used to call her Chicken Foot. When I met her, she told me she had gained weight from the decadence of American food, but she was still a little thing. Over the years, her body has become rounder with age. And life has left its scratches on her—because of bearing our children, because of life's hardships, because of the disease.

Here I have my stump. But when we are home, I go for walks. Past the houses of the other West Indians on the block— houses well kept, the small tidy space of lawns and tended flowers. Jacinth planted shrubs and flowers in alternating color arrangements in our yard. White people once lived in every house on our block. I don't know why West Indians picked Canarsie as the neighborhood to overtake. Now only one white person remains on our block, a woman obsessed with cats. Her house is the only one on the block without a yard of dirt and plants. Instead her yard is concrete and cats.

It's because of her that the strays on the block have one of their ears clipped to signify that they've been neutered. She has what looks like an old doghouse out in the yard for them. I don't know that any of them ever sleep in there but I see that they eat the provisions she puts out, a big tray of dry cat food and a bowl of milk and another one of water. This is the house that Jacinth says is the eyesore on the block. She says, "Di only kind of people weh live like dat are white people and African Americans." It's true that the ugly concrete and the house itself are nothing to look at twice. Twenty cats eating and drinking and licking each other behind the fence. When I walk by, most of them pause to look at me. Some immediately look away, while others hold my gaze. Sometimes when I drive down the street, I look around at the houses of the West Indians, the yards, the tidy lives we have built, and it surprises and impresses me.

Back in Brooklyn I walked whenever I didn't know what to do with myself—usually in the afternoon after lunch and sometimes after dinner if the sun goes down late. When I knew about the baby, and even after he came, it seemed like a dream, like a dirty piece of untruth someone told me. Even after I saw him with my own two eyes and felt him with my hands, I couldn't believe it. And I couldn't sleep for a long time after, maybe for a full year. I used to leave Jacinth's side to walk before the sun came up.

My son is on my mind. He is handsome, athletic, and smart. He is everything I could have wanted in a son, and his mother says the same. When I pictured the boy I wanted to raise, I imagined a boy better than I was, because in my mind I would have had an easier time if I had a father to show me the way. As a boy I wanted a man to teach me cricket, to show me how to fight. And as I got older, my needs became more complicated. I wanted a man to give me advice on how to live life. I wanted a man to love my mother. I wanted a man to show me how to remain faithful to my wife.

Today Junior turns sixteen. When Jacinth gave birth to our second daughter, I smiled as though I wasn't disappointed the baby wasn't a boy. If the doctor hadn't warned us against having any more children because of the difficulty of the pregnancy, if I couldn't see that Jacinth was content with two daughters, and if I could've handled the disappointment of a third daughter, I wouldn't have turned down Jacinth's suggestion that we try a third time. I knew she was only suggesting a third child for my happiness—she never wanted more than two children. And then I met my son's mother and even though it was something we planned against, she became pregnant. To have a son, I had to carry on with another woman, and I was convinced I could hear God laughing. Or maybe it was the devil laughing. It all felt like a cruel thing to happen to me. When I heard the news about the pregnancy, when I imagined my mother or wife or my daughters hearing, it filled me with a kind of sadness I wouldn't wish on the devil.

Once, my daughter Courtney told Jacinth about one of her college boyfriends. He was a Jamaican-American boy who took a bunch of pills to kill himself instead of allowing his family to find out about his homosexuality. Later, over dinner, Jacinth told me the story, explaining it was why Courtney was having difficulty at school, even dropping out of one of her classes. The story didn't make sense to me. I asked Jacinth, "So you mean this boy would attempt to kill himself over letting his family see that he's gay?" But when I found out about the pregnancy, when I thought how it would break Jacinth and when I thought about how it would cause my mother and my daughters to look at me differently, I considered for the first and only time that dying could be a relief from having to see their faces.

When possible, Jacinth turns her back when she's dressing or undressing so that I don't see the flatness where her breasts used to be. I don't know why she does this. I understand that she's shy for me to see, maybe it's that she doesn't want me to see the ugly scars or to think of her as unwomanly. But after all this time, I don't understand how she could feel the need to hide. One time I said to her, "Then, Jacinth, why you turn when you taking off your dress? A hide you a hide fram me? A see you don't want me to see you? I'm your husband. You don't have to hide from me." She looked surprised, as if she hadn't expected me to notice her newfound modesty. "I am not hiding anything," she said, but it sounded weak, she couldn't even make her lie convincing. Three years ago, when she felt the lump, she put my hand on her breast so I could feel it too because she hoped she was imagining things. After the surgery and during the chemotherapy, when I thought about her dying, and when I think about the cancer coming back and taking her, there is relief in thinking that

she might never know about Junior. That she could go thinking of me as a good man. My pride shames me.

The rusty nail clipper is already in my pocket when Jacinth
comes through the back door to call me for lunch. It is good
timing because my stomach has just started to complain.
When I get into the house, Jacinth is sitting in front of her
plate and Ugly is already eating. The smell of curry fills the
room. I look down to see that on my plate the curry chicken
is staining the white rice yellow. I'm only a little surprised to
see Ugly at our dining table. Sometimes I walk with him
down to the shop to play dominoes with the men in front.
Jacinth says that I have lost my age card, but she says this
while smiling. During the game, oftentimes Ugly and Richie
get into an argument, and Old Henry takes up his broom and
shoos us from the front of his shop. He poses the broom at
younger men, and he only shakes his head at me. I don't
know why he bothers. It doesn't take one hour for the men
to return to playing dominoes in front of his shop.

Ugly lives next door with a young girl. An Obeah man
used to live in their house. A man named Keston, who my
mother would smile at but throw away any food he gave us.
If my mother were alive, she would talk at the stupidity of
people moving into his house. Last year, the first time Jacinth
and I saw Ugly, we had walked down to the shop and while
Old Henry started putting our groceries in a plastic bag, he
started to call, "Ugly!" He must have called "Ugly!" five times
before a man appeared from the back of the shop. "Ugly, dese

people want a piece of yellow yam" Old Henry told him.
"Guh dig up one." Jacinth and I were shocked. We had heard
all manner of wicked names given to people—no other kind
of people is as wicked as Jamaicans when it comes to name-
calling. But we had never heard a man called Ugly to his face,
nor did we imagine that a man would answer to Ugly. That's
how our fascination with him began. And then we saw the
girl he lives with, a pretty little coolie girl, long-haired and
light-skinned. Ugly brought her and the baby to show off.
She came holding the baby in her hand, wearing a tight little
skirt, looking like somebody's daughter a grown man ruined.

When they left, Jacinth shook her head. "Then where
him find that gal now?"

"A same thing mi a wonder."

"Some a dem ya girls these days don't have no shame.
You tink mi would a follow back a one man wid no teeth
inna him mouth when mi was a young girl? Jesus. Something
name shame."

"Well, you know how dem say beauty is in the eye of the
beholder," I said, laughing.

"Wally, the man don't have one teeth inna him mouth.
Mi feel sorry fah di people who pickney him ruin. Yuh tink
that girl twenty? I can't even tink who nastier, the gal or
Ugly."

Ugly's main problem is that the girl can't cook. Every day
he eats with us, he reminds us. Today he says, "She try but
she nuh reach deh yet. Yestideh di dinner she cook would-
nah cum out too bad if she neva figet di food pon di fire. She

did a bathe di baby an she figet di food pon di fire." Jacinth and I always listen to him complain, Jacinth even offers him seconds, which he is always happy for, but after he leaves, we laugh at him. We dissect every foolish thing he says. It feels good to be accomplices. He realizes we love to hear him talk, and since he loves to hear himself, we get along wonderfully.

"Dat woman," he begins, but is distracted by a forkful of food.

We are waiting for him to continue. He barely talks about his wife. He always calls her "dat woman." The woman he left for the young girl. We've heard him complain about her—the money she wants, how miserable she is, and his belief that she is turning the children against him by calling him "dat slack man" in front of them.

"Dat woman really knew how fi love a Jamaican man."

"Why yuh sey dat, Ugly?"

"Because wat a man need more dan good food in him belly, a clean house, and someone fi hug up wid at night?"

But apparently this is not enough. Look at me, look at my father, who my mother cussed all the days of her life.

"Den yuh regret leaving her?"

"Too late fi tink 'bout dat."

Now that we've finished eating, Ugly leaves as quickly as he came. Jacinth goes to lie down, leaving me to wash up the dishes and the pots. When she climbs out of bed an hour later, I am sitting on the couch with my eyes closed, the newspaper spread out on my lap. I listen as she moves around the bedroom, changing her housedress to outside clothes, pulling a brush through her wig. Finally, she is climbing into her shoes that are sitting outside of the door. I open my eyes to see that she is looking at me.

"You want anything, Wally?"

"Yeah, bring me a cream soda."

When I hear her footsteps going down the steps in front of the house, I pull my cellphone and the phone card out of my pocket. My son answers his cellphone and his voice sounds newly mature to me. When he says, "Hi, Daddy," I hear in the music of his words that he is happy to hear from me. I don't have to ask where he is—the sound of many voices coming through, beneath his voice, paints a story for me. I see a tall, handsome boy, who looks barely anything like me except that we have the same feet and hands but his still glow with youth. He has his mother's face, a narrow, angular face that is more beautiful as a man's face. People have said he should look into modeling. I see my son floating through the school gate with the end of school crowd, his six-two height bobbing above the sea of teenagers. The school year has just started and he tells me that it's going well. He wants to hear me confirm that I will be back in New York in two weeks.

This is our second year coming back to Blackwoods. For as long as we can, our plan is to spend six months of the year on the island. This was always Jacinth's retirement dream, though now it feels crucial to her in case she doesn't have many years left. I told her I was happy to no longer deal with anyone else's business during my time off, by which I meant that I was happy we were closing down the free childcare ser-

vice our two daughters were accustomed to using and abus-
ing when school is out for our grandkids. But in the back of
my mind, I worried about my son, about leaving him for six
months in the year. When he said, "It's okay, Daddy," I listened and was disappointed to not hear resentment in his
voice.

I've walked to the edge of the front of our yard to look
down the road for Jacinth. I see her walking back up the hill,
a plastic bag in her hand. Every day, she walks down to the
shop to buy a gizzard and to chat up Mrs. Old Henry. She
will eat one half of the gizzard while she cooks dinner, and
the other half she will eat with a cup of ginger tea while we
are watching the evening news. My son tells me that his
mother and his stepfather are taking him for dinner and a
movie tonight. He thanks me for the money I sent and then
he is explaining that he has to go because his friends are waiting on him so that they can all take the train home together.
I say, "Happy birthday," I say, "Bye," then I am putting the
cellphone back into my pocket and walking down the road
to meet my wife. When I reach her, I will take the bag from
her and put my arm through her arm and we will walk home
together.

ON SHELF

Glenroy mentioned marriage the first time they talked on the phone, and at first Doreen had been flattered. He had said, "Yuh look like di type ah woman mi wan' fi marry," and Doreen had wondered how he knew this, when mostly all he knew about her was what he had gleaned from Facebook. It was true that her profile was in itself quite modest—only a few pictures: of her on an apple-picking trip with colleagues in her department, holding the branch of an apple tree heavy with fruit and smiling into the camera; with her best girlfriend (the two of them looking a decade younger); another with her mother, who looked into the camera unsmiling in her house clothes and her head tie, as though she was cooking and someone had pulled out a camera and her daughter had wrapped an arm around her neck, and all of it happening without her permission. Sometimes Doreen shared a Bible verse as her status. Last week: "Favor is deceitful, and beauty is vain: but a woman that feareth the LORD, she shall be praised—Proverbs 31:30." Fifteen people, including Glenroy, had liked her status. Sometimes she shared her triumphs: "I FINISHED the first chapter of my dissertation!!!!!!!!!!!!! Praise God." Eighteen people, including Glenroy, had liked her status.

She hadn't seen him in the ten years since she'd left Jamaica, and she hadn't known him when they'd lived in Jamaica. He'd only been a man she knew in passing, who she had seen with mutual friends. At the time, he had been married to Crystal, the woman who did Doreen's hair—a light-skinned woman with small hands, breasts that looked too big for her frame, and whose voice was high and sweet and kind. Doreen had come to see Crystal as the type of hairdresser she could trust—the kind who wouldn't cut too much off her hair because she was envious of customers with good hair. Doreen's last hairdresser had always cut too much hair, and too much off a woman Doreen knew, and had explained to the woman that long hair didn't fit fat women. Crystal played gospel music in her salon, which Doreen had admired as an excellent way of ministering to customers. They seemed ill matched to Doreen—Glenroy and Crystal did. He taught physical education at one of the local high schools, and looking at him a woman could tell that he spent time at the gym lifting weights. Doreen didn't understand how Crystal could believe that a man with arms like that could remain faithful to her. It didn't help that he was light-skinned with light-colored eyes, a color Doreen decided was what they called hazel. She'd overheard mutual friends talking about the high school girls who threw themselves at Glenroy, and how Glenroy had laughed when he told them about a recent incident as though the attention pleased him. "Of course he's fucking the young girls dem," one of the mutual friends, a man who sought after young girls, reasoned.

And so Doreen had been surprised when Glenroy sent her a friend request on Facebook, after he'd seen her profile on a mutual friend's page. He'd messaged her, "What's going on Doreen?" as casually as though they had ever been friends. She clicked through the photographs on his profile, wondering why she didn't see any of Crystal, when she remembered hearing that they had divorced. One message led to another: she was completing a PhD in Iowa City; he was working and living in Kansas City. It wasn't long before he suggested that they talk on the phone.

The last time Doreen was home, her friend's husband looked at her for a long moment and asked why she allowed herself to get on the shelf. "You're a good-looking woman," he told her with such conviction that she wondered if he believed that she needed to hear a compliment. She'd wanted to ask him if he really believed that she was the type of woman who wanted to be tied down with three little children and a worthless, bullfrog man like himself. Instead, she smiled and asked teasingly why he was troubling her. She knew that the husbands of her friends looked at her and desired her, or if they didn't desire her, they found her to be a more surprising woman than the ones they'd chosen to spend their lives with. When she should have been giving in to marriage and child-bearing, she had left a good job at a bank to pursue a master's and then a PhD in America. Doreen believed that because they wanted to remind her of her place, they brought up marriage. Or they brought up the exhausted status of her womb. Or they knew someone, an unmarried friend or a cousin, looking for a good woman to marry. Doreen couldn't help drawing satisfaction from comparing herself to her girl-friends back home. Many of them had grown fat after pro-ducing children, and all of them were overworked women who complained about their husbands. Doreen had kept her body right—she was hardly any bigger than she was in her twenties. People were always saying that she could easily pass for a much younger woman, which pleased her because beauty seemed more crucial than ever at her age.

It was a question she asked herself often: How had forty come and gone and she, Doreen Josephine Henry, was still unmarried? At 2 a.m. on a given weekday, when she was to teach at 8 a.m. that morning, it was the biggest mystery in the world. At her most optimistic self, she really did believe that eventually she would meet a man worth marrying and would have the daughter she had prophesied about from when she was a girl. She had long picked a name for the daughter: Sa-mantha. Could it be, she asked herself on these introspective nights, that she'd been too picky? When she lived back home, before she left to study in America, there had been many men who wanted to marry her. There was Alrick from church, who stuttered his affection to her. There was Gavin, who was shorter than she was, and she had reason to believe that he had a small penis. There were men like Winston, who drove a taxi and would be satisfied all the days of his life doing so. She hardly considered herself a superficial woman but she believed it important for a woman to have standards. All the men she had denied were long married with children.

The next day Glenroy called again. This time he seemed to have an agenda, asking question after question as though he were trying to fulfill some kind of interview process. He asked what Doreen had for dinner and that led to questions about the quality of her Jamaican cooking. He was pleased to hear that she'd cooked curry chicken recently, and then he complained, "Mi cyaan tek di pasta business. Dats why mi cyaan tek Yankee woman." Later, Doreen would know about the white woman he had dated and about the child she had miscarried. He had met the woman on the Internet, and had left Jamaica to be with her. She would learn that the woman liked to prepare bottled spaghetti sauce over noodles. And one day, out of curiosity, she will look the woman up on Facebook and be surprised to discover that she is very fat. This will surprise Doreen because once when she and Glenroy were watching a movie together, he had turned to her to say, "Yuh know, mi cyaan tek fat women," when the costar appeared on the screen. He had made up his face as though he smelled something bad, and Doreen had only looked at him. He turned his attention back to the television, but Doreen felt silently protective of fat women though she herself was not and had never been fat.

Doreen sometimes considered that what she needed to do was to find a nice white man to settle down with. The world found biracial children more beautiful than black children, and white men, though she'd never been involved with one, seemed sweet. They seemed like the kind of men to start preparing dinner if she came home late from work. But how to acquire one? In Iowa City, she had polite and at times vibrant conversations with white male classmates, but none of them had pursued her. The men in Iowa City—the white ones at least—were weird. If a Jamaican man wanted a woman, there was never any mystery about his desire. But in America, men, particularly white Midwestern men, often carried a less aggressive brand of approaching a woman. She'd shaken her head observing female classmates pursue men, or the halfhearted attempts of men too shy to boldly tell a woman that they wanted her.

And Doreen was well aware that she was a statistic—in America a highly educated black woman was the most likely demographic to remain unmarried or uncoupled after thirty. This gave her comfort—it was a reminder that there was nothing wrong with her, that it was just that there were obstacles against her beyond her control. Maybe she hadn't

been too picky. When she explained to two girlfriends in her
PhD program that this statistic was one of the strikes against
her, they had looked at her with the wide-eyed innocence of
white privilege.

Two months after the first phone call, Glenroy drove up
from Kansas. By then, Doreen had graduated from her PhD
program and was offered a one-year teaching appointment
with the university. He'd wanted to come sooner, almost de-
manding to come for her graduation, but Doreen made excuse after excuse, thinking it unwise to have a man she barely
knew meet her aging mother, who had flown from Jamaica
for the ceremony. She also didn't want him to think that she
was easy. When she opened up the door for their first meeting wearing a new dress and sandals that showed off her
freshly painted pink toenails, she was underwhelmed, but
she fixed her face into a smile so as not to show it. The years
of their absence from each other, as well as flattering Facebook photographs, had allowed her to anticipate a more
beautiful man. In person he looked older, shorter, and though
his arms were still muscular, he now had a slight beer belly.
Fortunately, his face was still handsome. He was one of those
Jamaicans whose European blood was evident in his hazel-
green eyes, straight nose, and fair skin. He even had freckles
scattered over his nose. His English was horrible, and this
was one flaw Doreen couldn't overlook—she had to ask him
again how long he had been living in America, because seven
years seemed too long to be unable to speak a sentence with-

out patois. That first day when he misunderstood something she said and picked her up and took her to the bedroom, she had been so aroused that she almost let him undress her. But she worried that if sex happened, she wouldn't be the kind of woman he wanted to marry. And what a bore he was: he didn't want to go into town to eat what he called "white people food," he wasn't interested in going to see a movie because it was a "waste of money," and when Doreen finally convinced him to let her show him around town, he thought that the pair of shorts she put on were too short. "Yuh wear dem kinds of tings?" he asked her, and later she would regret her decision to change into a sundress that hit her knee.

Glenroy was open about the kinds of women he didn't like: loud women, it seemed, were the worst type. "A woman no have fi huff an' puff fi get a point across," he once explained. There was a show Doreen enjoyed watching that starred a loud black woman, and Glenroy suggested that she change the channel, saying he couldn't stand listening to the woman. It seemed personal, this dislike for loud women, and so Doreen wondered where he had encountered such a woman. She couldn't imagine that Crystal had ever spoken too forcefully to him. From what she was able to gather about his mother, she was a no-nonsense hurricane of a woman, so perhaps it was a similar force he was running from. He also didn't like slack women—the kind of women who behaved as though they were men, freely giving in to fucking and baby-making as though it was all an afterthought. His sister was this type of woman, and he was always, as Jamaicans say, crying shame after her. "Di last time mi go a Jamaica," he once explained to Doreen over the phone, "I look at her an' ask her two questions. I asked her if she 'ave sense and then I asked her if she 'ave a ting name shame." "What did she say?" Doreen wanted to know. She expected to hear that a fight broke out between them. Glenroy made Peggy seem like a brute of a woman with her four baby fathers, and, once, she had fought another woman for a man in public. Glenroy explained, "Wha' she could a sey? All she couldah do a cry." He didn't like women with false hair, false eye-lashes, or false nails.

Doreen wondered how much of herself she could divulge to him. She had been with more than a few men. She didn't consider herself promiscuous, but she had long accepted that she liked having sex. And she knew that if she had told Glenroy any of this, told him about the African custodian who cleaned her department and who she let fuck her on her desk a few times, he would think her a different kind of woman. During their first conversation on the phone, he'd told her, "Yuh seem like a decent woman," and because it was a compliment, she was flattered. But she wasn't exactly sure what he meant by "decent," and if she asked, it could betray her for who she really was. When Glenroy had asked how many men she had been with, she responded with, "I've had two boyfriends," which was and wasn't a lie. When she turned the question to him, he thought about it for a moment before he confessed, "You know, I don't know." And he had smiled slyly, as though he might as well have been flexing his muscles or showing her the length and width of his penis.

And on a sleepless weeknight, say 3 a.m. on a Monday, marriage itself was a mystery to her. She could barely think of any of her friends who were happily married. Even the ones who pretended to be happy would slip and betray their unions for what they really were. Her mother, who had in the last year looked at Doreen and asked if she was "one ah those woman who say dem dey wid woman," had raised Doreen and her siblings by herself when her common-law husband left them for another woman he would eventually follow to England. Doreen knew that her brother wasn't faithful to his wife. When she really thought about it, what was marriage besides a savior from lifelong loneliness? And one could marry and still remain lonely.

Sometimes at 3 a.m., thoughts of marriage were less interesting than this thing people called love. How were people, she wondered, so sure that what they felt was love? And what did love feel like? She watched reality dating shows in part to understand, but besides feeling entertained by the heated exchanges between the tanned, thin women and the conventionally attractive men, all the contestants white, all of them so hungry for a soulmate, love only seemed desperate and kind of sad, because although there was the lucky man and woman and the diamond ring purchased by the network, there were all the other contestants who went home empty-handed.

There were fleeting moments when she felt strongly for

Glenroy. His eyes were so pretty; a green-brown stunning and warm that reminded her of sunlight. He made her laugh— channeling the world through the gaze of his Jamaican up- bringing. He could be sweet, bringing her a dozen mangoes or a dozen roses and a bottle of wine when he came to see her. These moments were thrilling, but they were as fragile as spiderwebs because in one moment Glenroy wasn't too bad and maybe she could imagine loving him, but then in the next moment he reminded her that he was a man who couldn't speak proper English. She wondered if this was the nature of love—if it wasn't a feeling as determined and con- tinuous as the world made it seem. She felt that it was a ques- tion she was too old to still be asking.

Maybe she'd been in love once. If love is ever present, a cycle as rhythmic as the sun and the moon, she'd been in love once. There was Winston from primary school—as chil- dren they had played together, and later in high school, they were friends. He'd always been a sensitive, reasonable boy, the kind of man women like to confide in. He was the son of a farmer, often helping in his father's grounds after school. He'd been her first when she was seventeen. Many a time she'd met him at the grounds in the early evening, his clothes filthy and his skin smelling like toil, but making love this way, lying together in the bushes, made the whole thing more exciting. The first year she left for college in Kingston, she made up her mind that she deserved a higher class of man, not the kind of man who came home from work with dirt under his fingernails. Later, when she returned to teach at one of the local high schools, there were numerous opportunities when she could have looked meaningfully at him and told him that after all he was the man that she wanted. All those years he had remained at the periphery, and although there were other men who passed through her life and other women who passed through his, it was clear to the both of them that he was only waiting on the word from her because as a young man he had decided that she was the woman he would love. Whenever she considered his devotion, the fact that his dream girl at nine and at twenty-five was the same woman, the narrowness of his scope, the lack of imagination, displeased her. It further proved that he was too simple a man. It would have been different if he'd traveled, educated himself, and seen what the world of women had to offer and came back for her. Now, that would have been romantic. For two years, she was certain that she was to marry a man who was to become a doctor, but nearing the end of their second year together, he moved to Cuba to study. It took her long to recover from the fact that he hadn't wanted her to go with him and that he wasn't interested in a long-distance relationship. It would be a full year before another man touched her.

Finally, Winston married another woman, and gave her three girl children. Whenever Doreen went back home and they linked up, he would ask in a teasing astonishment, "You still nuh marry?" "No man good enough for you," he had told her on her last visit, and though he was smiling and it was to appear that he was only teasing her, there was a deliberate heaviness to his words, a history to them, a told-you-so, and they stayed with Doreen for a long time.

• • •

Sex with Glenroy, when it finally came, was surprisingly good. They played the game men and women sometimes play—Glenroy wanted it more, and Doreen was modest, and eventually with time, that being his third visit to Iowa City, he was able to seduce her. They had been surprised by the other's passion. "How it go?" he had asked after the first time. "Oh," he said remembering, "a lady inna di streets an' a freak inna di sheets." With the African man, Doreen had initiated things. She saw him and guessed that he might have a big penis, and it had been a really long time for her, so she had strategized the series of events that would find them alone in the department after everyone else had gone home for the evening. They'd only stopped because he told her that he was to be married to a woman from back home who was soon to move to America. Weeks later, while squeezing the mangoes on sale at Walmart, Doreen saw the African custodian out of the corner of her eyes. He was with a woman wearing a hijab, who was picking out onions. When he looked over and saw Doreen, he turned his face away quickly. Later when Doreen saw him sweeping the department floor, she asked why he hadn't said hello at Walmart and he'd said that he hadn't seen her, and this caused her to laugh long and loud and he made up his face and moved away from her. After that, whenever they saw each other, they pretended as though they didn't know each other.

"Glenroy knows how to use his penis," she told a girlfriend back in Jamaica over the phone, and they had both laughed because it was the only good thing Doreen had ever said about him.

Six months after the first phone conversation, Glenroy was driving from Kansas City to Iowa City every other week. Doreen kept going back and forth questioning what she was doing with him, and whether she was only with him to fill the time before a man of better substance, one who was more intellectually engaging, came along. In Iowa City, the pickings of eligible black men were slim, and she felt invisible to other races. Mostly she believed that for the time being she couldn't do any better than Glenroy. But he could be sweet. He found her sexy, and frequently told her so. And there were moments when they were naked after sex when she thought that she might be able to love him. He would wrap one arm around her and they would talk about life back home—about people they both knew, about the state of the country, about their mothers who were still making life in Jamaica. They would laugh at so-and-so foolish person, at their younger selves, at the ignorance and arrogance and the hilarity of Jamaicans. Sometimes, it seemed that he'd saved her from the loneliness of the Midwest. She never felt more connected to him than when they were talking about Jamaica. What ever happened to so-and-so person? she might ask. And he would explain that the person was now married and living in Canada, or moved to another parish, or the same as they remembered him. "Life in Jamaica sweet," Glenroy would say, would always say, and Doreen would agree because it was true. They were of the same generation, the ones who had left the Caribbean as adults for better lives, and they would spend the rest of their years making comparisons, making complaints, but when they thought about it, when they really considered it, every road led to America. They would build retirement homes in Jamaica.

"T'ree months from now we start talk marriage," Glenroy had said after six months together, and Doreen had been so shocked by his presumption that she didn't say anything. She smiled as though she was pleased.

People back home didn't understand why Doreen was still in school—she didn't bother explaining everything that went into completing a PhD in economics, because it would have fallen on dunce ears. For some of her friends, her ambition impressed and amused them and at times provoked envy. "Eh eh! Look at the economist," a friend breastfeeding her child said in a teasing way, when Doreen walked into her yard. Another friend looked at Doreen in a funny way and asked, "You nuh want fi have a baby?" She had said yes and hadn't betrayed that if having a child was a possibility, she would have long ago crossed this goal off her list. And now even Glenroy was concerned with her uterus. "Aftah we marry, yuh ha fi hurry an' get pregnant," he'd told her.

From when she was a little girl, Doreen had wanted to learn, and a degree in economics seemed like a practical choice. She believed that an education was what would separate her from her mother and her mother's mother, women

who lived such meager lives. In Iowa, her classmates talked of
the cornfields as a way to signify that this was the kind of
place their education had stolen them away to, but for Doreen
the cornfields opened up her life to possibility, and anyway
the cornfields were far enough away from town that she forgot
about them until she got on the bus that took her the four
hours to Chicago, where a friend from back home lived. It was
disappointing to learn that Iowa City could give her little besides an education—she had hoped to also meet a man, to
marry, to have a child. Iowa was to take five years of her life,
but she had already decided that she wouldn't miss the place.
Soon she was to begin the process of applying for jobs at universities across the country, because by next summer her
teaching fellowship would have ended. It had crossed her
mind that if she didn't get a job for next fall, and university
jobs were competitive, marrying Glenroy would be another
way to stay in America legally, because by then her visa would
have expired. With legal status, she would keep reapplying for
jobs, and eventually realize the dream of becoming a tenure-
track professor. Glenroy, it seemed, might be able to give her a
few of the things she wanted. But at what cost? she often asked
herself. What was the cost of marrying a less than ideal man?

Doreen had wondered but she didn't have the chance to ask
because Glenroy was open about why his marriage to Crystal
failed. The first time they met in person, he said that Crystal
was nasty. "She wouldn' clean. Nuh even her drawers," he
said. And then he explained how time and time again he had

found bloody panties under the bed. "It easy fi cheat pon a woman when yuh cyaan respeck her," Glenroy said, before explaining that cheating wasn't in his nature but that no man wants to make love to his woman in a nasty house. He would go on to say that he suspected that something was wrong with Crystal, that she wasn't too right in the head.

For a long time, Doreen wouldn't know that Glenroy was living with a woman and her children when he started visiting her in Iowa City. He'd left the fat woman, who brought him to America, for someone else, and had left the second woman for Doreen. He had tried a white woman and an African American, and realized that what he needed was a woman from back home. Doreen wouldn't know any of this for a long time, and at first she was angry, but after some time she would wonder if every marriage wasn't even a little convenient, because by then the baby was fat and pretty. When the little girl looked in her eyes in the soft way that young enough children look and look as though they are searching and seem to have found the person who can explain how the warm moist cave of a womb can become such a different world, it mattered even less to Doreen that her marriage managed to stand on the flimsy foundation she had for so long refused, deeming herself better than. When the child, who indeed she named Samantha, looked at her like that, it seemed that perhaps marriage was after all not the worst idea, and if it was, she reminded herself that a woman as resourceful as herself had options.

WE EAT OUR DAUGHTERS

My mother had two faces and a frying pot
where she cooked up her daughters
into girls
before she fixed our dinner.
My mother had two faces
and a broken pot
where she hid out a perfect daughter
who was not me
I am the sun and moon and forever hungry
for her eyes.

—AUDRE LORDE, "From the House of Yemanjá"

Corrine

The morning of the day my mother left my father for the first time, she played her Bob Marley records on his beloved record player. Back then my favorite song was "I Shot the Sheriff" and hers was "Is This Love." We played and re-played our favorite songs, my mother adding to the coffee cups in the sink, and after lunchtime, she threw the record player and her wedding ring out the window, and finally, we got into a cab with the suitcase she had packed. What is it about first times? I remember that morning with the vibrancy of yesterday, but all the other times we left my father are memories that blur together.

As a child, I used to examine my mother's Bob Marley records. Why was she in love with him when she couldn't stand my father? He was unkempt compared to my father, who believed that black people should be tidy so as not to draw negative attention. I decided that I was in love with Bob Marley too. This was why, when I met Christopher years later at a coffee shop in Berkeley, I joked that he was the ghost of Bob Marley, a reincarnation, my white boy, the lead singer of a reggae band when he wasn't writing his dissertation on William Faulkner. And I, his Rita Marley—the joke went—without the infidelity.

The day we met, I was sipping tea in a coffee shop while I read for one of my classes. I noticed the white man sitting next to me because he was nearly impossible to miss—his blond dreads were halfway down his back. I had forgotten about him until he leaned over to ask if I was enjoying my book.

Now, I wonder if we would've become anything more than an encounter in a coffee shop if I hadn't told him that I was Jamaican-born. This small fact, and I could tell that I'd become more interesting. What could a man brought up in an upper-middle-class family find to adore in a small island? Plenty. "Fuck resorts," he told me that first day, and then he made an argument comparing tourism to colonialism that he'd had plenty of time to think about. His first trip to Jamaica he'd gone with Lindon, a friend from his undergraduate years at Harvard, an international student who invited Christopher into his family's humble home. Sometimes I wonder what Christopher had been looking for, because if he hadn't been looking for something, if his upbringing hadn't been lacking in some way, he wouldn't have nailed the island to the cross. I could never understand, as his parents and siblings were kind and loving enough. He saw that his classmate's family didn't have the kind of money his family had to squander—Christopher's mother could walk into a shop because she felt like buying a new dress. When night fell, he and Lindon smoked herb and drank rum behind the chicken coop, and he was inspired by the clean air, the stars above, and the night's darkness, thick and consuming and in this way unlike any night he had ever experienced. Of course, only ten days in Jamaica and he had managed to encounter a local beauty, who he talked to on the phone for six months until things simmered down.

He didn't become a devout Rastafarian until a few years into our marriage. He asked that I stop relaxing my hair, and instead of pants, I should wear long skirts. At first these demands didn't feel like demands. They felt like requests, so I obliged. He asked why I continued to eat meat when I knew the benefits of a plant-based diet, and because this made sense, I cooked vegetarian meals for us, and for the children when they came along.

"When yuh a guh lef' dat madman?" my mother wants to know, whenever we talk on the phone. She says that I married a white man who doesn't know the color of his skin. She says that it's one thing to be with a Jamaican man who wants to run her life, which is referring to her preserved though unhappy marriage to my father without explicitly stating it, but that it's another, worse thing to have a white man run my life. She says that her home is available when I'm ready to leave. I want to ask her, "Do you remember the first time we left? Don't you remember that we kept coming back?" But there are certain questions a daughter doesn't ask, and moreover, the past is the past now that she is almost content with my father, now that he is too old to beat her.

This morning I get up as usual to blend the vegetables and fruits Christopher likes to drink for breakfast. He walks into the kitchen as the blender is going, and when he kisses the back of my neck, I turn around briefly to catch his blue eyes. For a moment, and there have been a million moments like these, I wish that he was just a white man comfortable with everything the world has and hasn't given him. He pushes his dreadlocks out of his face, he pulls a glass from the cabinet and pours a glass of water, and I watch him.

Renee

There is a way to be cruel that seems Jamaican to me. But I've heard other islanders say the same thing, so maybe it's a Caribbean thing. Though Africans and African Americans tell me that it's a similar way with them, so maybe it's a black thing. It's saying exactly what you think, regardless of how it will affect the listener. Perhaps this is the language of the oppressed—the colonized, the enslaved. Maybe our kind doesn't have time for soft words. My friend, from Jamaica same as me, says that she prefers this to people talking behind her back. I don't know that I agree.

I knew that something wasn't normal—or at least I suspected it. But I didn't think of the words "eating disorder" until a therapist said it to me in my early twenties, and then I kept the words to myself because no one I knew would understand. And also: How to explain that I had an American disease, a white woman's disease?

There. We used to live there. Chester Street, but I've forgotten the house number. I could go look, but my body doesn't feel like moving from this bus stop. See how that corner of Chester is a fried chicken spot now? I can't remember what it used it be, but I want to believe it was another neighborhood grease spot, maybe Chinese. The other corner is the Associated supermarket. When I turn my head to look in its direction, it is as though I'm turning my head to look at history. The history I remember is my sister, my brother, and me walking behind my mother—she was still our mother hen then—on Saturday evenings to buy something special we ate while we watched television. Now, who should exit the supermarket but the man who lived and maybe still lives in the house next door. He nods my way and says "Hello," but it has been twelve years since we moved and I can't tell if he recalls my face. I haven't forgotten him, young-looking and handsome, as if he hasn't aged at all, brown-skinned like the president. You know how there are people who don't know you but you know them? You've been watching them

long enough so that if they bent their head over the bed
you're dying in when old age finally licks you, and even
though your eyes aren't what they used to be, you recognize
them almost as clearly as you recognize the man you've been
loving for longtime or the children you pushed from inside
you. I couldn't forget him because I memorized his ways for
the two years we lived on Chester Street. I saw him every day
walking the streets, always neatly dressed and stopping to say
hello to everybody, helping old women carry their bags. That
kind of guy. If you didn't know that drugs messed up his
head and that's what keeps him polite and simple, you would
see his ways and hear what he has to say and wonder what
he's doing in Brownsville with these other street boys.

Back then we lived in a basement apartment on Chester
Street. We had been staying with my mother's friend, who
was settled on Flatbush, since she had the sense to leave the
island years earlier when everything was easier—you would
have your green card in less time in those days, no waiting for
twelve years, "till kingdom come." Those days America
wasn't tired of foreigners yet.

We'd slept on an old mattress in my mother's friend's
living room. It was hot—we'd got off the plane in August—
and the air conditioners were only in the bedrooms. From
a corner of the living room, a fan blew hot air. My brother
could sleep shirtless, since he didn't have to worry about my
mother's friend's sons watching him sleep half naked. This is
why, after three months of all four of us on that mattress, the
basement apartment felt like home to me. Even after I heard
my mother marvel to her friend that coming to America was

moving backwards since we had to start from the bottom. So I realized that where we lived was somewhere to be ashamed of. We had left a house with front and back yards and a dog named Lady for concrete playgrounds, a mattress in someone else's apartment, and, finally, a basement apartment. Because I was still so young, I often forgot to feel ashamed.

I remember the basement apartment like this: down the steps was a living room so small it could only fit a two-seater and a television, but my siblings and I didn't mind sitting on the carpeted floor to watch our shows. Then it was my mother's room, followed by a room big enough for a kitchen area, a small dining table, and a bookshelf. I remember how one time my siblings and I ate scrambled eggs and white rice at the table, and another time we ate fried chicken from the Chinese food restaurant. I think we ate the fried chicken on my birthday.

Because my brother was small enough, he slept with my mother, while my sister and I shared a bed in the other bedroom, which was past the kitchen. We weren't allowed in the front yard because my mother said that the people next door sold drugs. The place we came from, we had heard the rumor that terrible things could happen to children, but this kind of thinking was primarily absent from our consciousness.

My mother worked at a daycare, where an old white lady used to come and show the children her guinea pigs, and allow them one at a time to hold out a piece of lettuce or a carrot. Because the old lady's son threatened to put her in a nursing home if she didn't do something about her guinea pigs always having babies, she started to give the babies away, which is how we came to own two guinea pigs when we lived on Chester Street. I don't know what happened to those guinea pigs. I know we couldn't have given them away, because we adored them, but I also don't remember that they died. They used to bite our fingers if we weren't careful when feeding them carrots. I remember that they had sharp teeth.

I turn my head from the Associated supermarket to see that the B35 is letting on the last few passengers. History always has a way of weighing me down, making me forget myself, forget the present. The therapist had wanted to know when my trouble with food and my body began, and we narrowed it down to my moving to America. It's so tricky to name the beginning of things, to see an experience for what it is, but I remember being fourteen years old and being afraid of what food could do. The food in public school was fatty and processed, and students didn't walk or run in the yard during lunchtime like we used to back home. We sat in the cafeteria and talked. I remember knowing that I had the potential to be more beautiful, and that this wasn't just my opinion but the opinion of others as well. My family—my mother and aunts and uncles—wanted to talk about my body whenever they saw me because I'd gained a lot of weight. It was out of concern, but how to explain how assaulted I felt? How to explain the shame I felt when my mother singled me out to explain to a church member that no, she didn't want any more cookies to take home because she didn't want Renee to gain more weight? The years passed. My family continued talking.

The move itself had been dramatic, my mother taking us

without our father's permission because he'd lost interest in being a husband and father. My mother made up her mind quickly—one moment I was preparing to start at an all-girls' high school in Jamaica, and it seemed that the next moment I was enrolled in a public school in Brooklyn. The therapist had wanted to know the disorder's origin story, but all I had were bits of memory: the time I finally had a little money to myself and binged on the Chinese food I bought in the neighborhood and then I wanted the food to go somewhere else that wasn't inside me; the time my aunt offered to buy us ice cream when the truck came around and then told me that if she was my size she wouldn't eat ice cream. Maybe beginnings aren't beginnings, maybe they are harder to pin down, like waves pulling off the shore at different moments, waves of all sizes and strengths, but eventually and ultimately they are all the same wide expanse of sea. I run to catch the bus before the doors close.

Yolande

I tell my roommate, Emma, a white girl who calls herself a poet, and who stands in our kitchen wearing a T-shirt that says "Abortion rights are human rights" and a pair of panties with pink roses, a cup of coffee in her hands, that my life will be my own when my mother is dead. I just got off the phone with my mother, who spent a large portion of our phone call in disbelief that one of her friends was organizing the wedding reception for her pregnant daughter and the low-life man who impregnated her. My mother had said, "Mi nuh know how some parent condone any an' any behavior." Emma's curly black hair is hanging long and loose, and she rests the coffee cup on the counter so that she can gather all of it into a bun on the top of her head. Meanwhile, I am trying to piece the words together to explain that of course if my mother dies tomorrow I would feel devastated, but I would also feel free. I know I won't be the first or the last person to whom the death of a loved one comes as a tragedy and an answer to a prayer at the same time. But Emma is looking like she wants to cry. When she talks to her mother on the phone, they have an actual conversation, sharing intimacies, thoughts both mundane and extraordinary. Once, Emma told me that when at sixteen she got her first serious boyfriend, her mother said to her, "So we need to get you on birth control." My own mother might really believe I'm a thirty-year-old virgin. Of course Emma can't help feeling sorry for me, and of course I regret that I've shared something she couldn't possibly understand. I stop talking mid-sentence because it doesn't make any difference to continue and she nods her head as though she understands. We sip our coffee, she attempts and fails to commiserate with me, and then we retire to our bedrooms.

It's funny to think that I came to America to study Caribbean literature. Now that I'm pursuing my PhD, even after all these years that my mother has seen that all I want to do is read, that all I've ever wanted to do is read, since it feels like the thing God made me to do, she still wants me home with her. If I was home, she could show me off to people, telling them that American schools gave me scholarships to study. If I was home, she would have someone to go to church with, even though unbeknownst to her I think that the Bible is the most imaginative book of fiction ever written. If I was home, we could take early morning walks—my mother's attempt to get back the "sexy body" her fifties took from her—with her telling me the hilarious, heartbreaking things that happen to her woman friends, the morning air in Mandeville as crisp and as sweet as fall in New York. Often, when we talk on the telephone, because I graduate in the spring, she asks what kinds of jobs are available in Jamaica for someone with a PhD in Caribbean literature. "Maybe I can teach at UWI," I tell her, even though unbeknownst to her, I am applying for tenure-track teaching jobs in the United States. In my mind, I will return to Jamaica for visitations as long as my mother is alive. When she is dead, I imagine that the island will feel less like home because there won't be anyone to return for.

Sometimes, I think that if my mother had a husband or a boyfriend, it would be different. Sometimes, I tease her that she should marry and she says, "Fi wha'?" The marriages of her women friends have disillusioned her. When she became pregnant out of wedlock, my father, an older man in the community, agreed to marry her, but when the day came, he didn't show up. This seems to be a pattern with him, because he mostly continued to fail to show up when I was growing up. Once, when one of my mother's friends invited her boy-friend to live with her and her children, my mother remarked to me that she didn't understand how a woman could bring a strange man into a house with her daughters. Sometimes, I wonder if for all these years she has been single for my sake, and if this is indeed the case, how to repay such a sacrifice?

When I told my mother about my last boyfriend, Dylan, she asked, "Why yuh don't come home an' meet ah nice Jamaican man? Yuh would really want fi wake up to a pair ah blue eyes every mawning?" But Dylan's eyes aren't blue; they're the same color as mine: brown. I hadn't told her about the other boyfriends I've had in America because it would reveal too much: she would guess I am sexually active; she would worry that a man would distract me from studying and maybe even become the reason I stay here. I told her about Dylan because I couldn't help it. Love had the effect of making me loose-lipped. With him I'd imagined a future—a few times after sex we'd become excited and talked about having children together. I said to my mother, "I have a boyfriend," and there had been a slight pause and then she continued with the story she was telling.

"Did you hear me? I said I have a boyfriend."

"I hear yuh," she said, and besides asking about his race, that seemed to be the extent of her interest in him. She continued to nudge me about the possibility of a "nice Jamaican man."

We've talked in passing about the possibility of her moving to America. But she doesn't have the qualifications to teach elementary school in America, and she says that she doesn't want to die here. This year my mother turned sixty, which means that she isn't leaving the only country she's ever known.

In America I meet women like Emma, whose mothers don't want anything from them besides knowing that they are happy. It seems that mine believes that her happiness and my happiness are one and the same. She lives as if she believes that even after all this time an invisible umbilical cord connects us. And for my part, I am afraid of not being who she wants me to be. Jamaican mothers raise their daughters to be obedient, and some of us don't know how to be any other way even when we are women. Some of us Jamaican daughters too easily forget the days our mothers were most tender. They tied ribbons in our hair that matched the colors of the clothes we wore. We were as beautiful as flowers. We are never as beautiful as we were then. We have the photographs as proof. And we do need proof because as women we are at times resentful daughters, who can barely remember the days our mothers treated us as innocently as we once were.

My mother used to warn me, "Don't expect mi fi come ah yuh wedding if yuh marry any an' anybody," and I believed her. And so when Dylan and I ended things amicably, for all of the conversations about timing and how our separate futures didn't seem to merge, afterwards I couldn't help wondering if a part of me had been unavailable all along.

Cherry

Long before I knew my mother, there was a time when she was promiscuous. My sister Monique jokes that she also has white liver—a high libido. She tells me that she wants it every night, and her husband sometimes says a little seriously that he's not sure that he can keep up with her. Maybe this is the kind of thing that runs in a family, which could mean that white liver, a love of sex, would account for my mother's behavior. I know I love sex too, discovered this late, at thirty-seven, only this past summer when I met Afia and seriously considered for the first time that I was a lesbian. How else to explain that my heart opened like a bud? Here was Afia with her lisp, her big white teeth, and her high forehead—there was nothing and everything extraordinary about her. This kind of love is dangerous because you're always looking around, waiting for it to end. You're disillusioned enough to know that so few of us can keep something like that going.

In this world it's one thing for a woman to be promiscuous, and with the lovers I've had, I have no desire to judge. But it's another thing to allow several men to father your children. That's the kind of thing slack, shameless women do. What does it say about me that I prefer to believe that my mother was a woman so full with the desire to love that she took five different men into her bed, eventually bearing all seven of us?

Yet when I knew my mother, she didn't seem particularly interested in love or sex, and in fact she never had a kind word to say about any man besides Jesus Christ. I was the last child she gave birth to, the last child for another man who wouldn't marry her, a man who had spread his seed all over the district. I wonder if my mother might have been different before I knew her, so I ask my siblings if they remember her any differently. "Mama was always Mama," Smithy says, and everyone else more or less echoes the same sentiment. Maybe we weren't watching closely enough. In my teenage years, when my shape started to form, my mother told me in a prideful way that I had taken after her. Now, all these years later, it seems that that moment had hinted at her sexuality. She had been desirable and she had known it.

Last week, I saw Afia in a bookstore, and although there were a hundred things I wanted to say to her, including, "How could you have left me for a white woman?" I told her that Mama had passed away. "Oh no," she said, pulling me into a hug, and I couldn't help crying for all kinds of reasons, including the fact that Afia always manages to smell so good.

And as snobby as my mother was, I could never understand the type of men she allowed to lay on top of her. After all, she used to tell me which classmates she didn't want me hanging around with. The men she had children with are the kind of men I wouldn't answer to if they called out to me on the street. None of them are particularly handsome. They are the kind of men who don't hold any respectable jobs. They will pick up work wherever they can, maybe to help a man dig up a farm or lay cement, just enough money so that they can retire back to the rum shop or to play dominoes in front of the shop. Sometimes, I wonder what my father or the fathers of my brothers and sisters could have told my mother to seduce her. I can't imagine that any of them would know how to tell a woman compliments as beautiful as poetry. They are the kind of men who use the same lines for every woman, and I can't see my mother being naïve enough to believe tired words from a man. The woman I knew, no one, man or woman, would think to tell her any and any thing, because she would chase them off. But then I have to consider that perhaps raising seven children with little help from the fathers turned my mother into the woman I knew.

"You're going to let your mother shame you for your sexuality when she had seven children with five different men?" And so when Afia told me about the white woman, the first thing I wondered was whether I wasn't gay enough. There were books I hadn't read, sexual acts I hadn't done, and most telling, I was almost forty and wasn't out to my mother yet. "My little gay baby," Afia had said once at the beginning, but evidently that was cute for only a season.

When I was fifteen or sixteen, my mother started to eye me suspiciously. She would talk about how she didn't want certain "goin' ons" happening in her house. By now, all of my brothers and sisters were big men and women who had gone off into the world, and so I was the only one who still lived at home. Around this time, I started to feel that I was a big woman. My mother and I quarreled often. I believed that she wanted to run my life. Once she told me, "Just because yuh 'ave a big woman body don't mean dat yuh a big woman." I grew to mistrust her. I realized that she wasn't but a few years older than me—she had been nineteen—when she became pregnant for the first time and yet she wanted to treat me like a child. It hurt that she insinuated that I was sexually active when I wasn't. Just because she had been slack didn't mean that I was the same. Often when my mother was harsh with me, particularly when she talked about "goin' ons," I'd wanted to remind her of who she used to be.

When I graduated from high school, I started working at a bank in town. One day after work, I was passing by the rum shop when I heard my father call my name through the window. I continued to walk past the shop, and when he saw this, he came outside to call my name. I turned around. "Yuh can mek mi hold one hundred dollars?" he asked. He was drunk, holding on to the door for support. I looked at my father, this man who had given my mother two children before he gave a child to the woman who lived next door. That day I kissed my teeth and I walked away. He called after me and eventually he gave up, or I'd walked far enough so that his voice couldn't carry to me.

When I left Jamaica, I used to have to work myself up to call my mother. She complained that my siblings and I didn't call her often enough. She complained that she had seven ungrateful children. She complained that she worked hard enough as mother and father to receive any less than a call from at least one of us every day of the week. She said that she could die alone in the house and none of us would know. The questions about my life were sparse. Sometimes I called her and she told funny, vivid stories about so-and-so person from church or so-and-so person who lived in the community, and times like these I knew I loved her. But other times it was exhausting to hear how my siblings and myself had failed her.

I remember how one time I was talking to my older brother, complaining that while my mother wanted us to call her more often, she didn't make it easy for us to want to talk to her. We were sitting at his dining table, eating the saltfish and dumplings I cooked for breakfast. His wife was on the couch, where I slept at night, breastfeeding the baby. I had been in New York for only six months. I had a brother and sister in Canada, two brothers and one sister in America, and I had a sister still living in Jamaica. I came because I didn't have anything keeping me home. My mother had asked, "Yuh really ah lef' mi?" when I told her that I was moving to New York. She asked, "So who goin' tek care ah mi inna mi old age?" My sister Trisha, the only one to remain in Jamaica, lived on the other side of the island. At this point, my mother was barely past sixty. I never understood why death and old age were always at the front of her mind.

That day eating breakfast with my brother, he told me that he was going to come clean with our mother, telling her that no one told her to have so many children. Why, he asked me, looking at me so intently that for a moment I thought he wanted an answer, would she have all these children to complain about caring for them? "No one," he said, "tell her fi mek so much pickney." I laughed. Many times these words had been at the tip of my tongue. But I was raised in a country where children are taught to speak respectfully to their parents, so I held my words. My brother held his too.

• • •

Because pain, regret, and loss have a way of overlapping, a way of reminding one of the other, I think about Afia and I wonder what the term "love of my life" would mean to my mother. Or I think about my mother and I wonder what would she have said if I told her that I finally found love and with a woman. What if I had told her that after all this time and after so many men, those feelings in love songs, those feelings I had long doubted, had finally happened to me? What if I showed her how in our own way we were both deviances?

When my mother dies, she is a little over seventy. And she is alone in that house where she raised all seven of us. The stroke came surprisingly. Luckily, she dies on a Sunday, the day I always call her. When she doesn't answer, I worry without having a reason. It's how people say that God whispers warnings to us. I call and call, and eventually I call the neighbor and ask her to check on my mother. It is as though my mother is taunting me from the grave—she dies alone, like she always said that she would. It's true that my siblings and I are ungrateful, but we are ordinary, only ungrateful in the ways all daughters and sons are ungrateful. We called when we could. We sent money, gifts, even our children for summer vacations. My sisters and two of my brothers cry when we bury our mother. That mystery of a woman.

SHIRLEY FROM A SMALL PLACE

Part 1

Earlier that day, she'd been a mermaid. There'd been a merman. They'd kissed underwater, wrapping their fins together, their faces pinched in agony—the director had instructed, "Look like you're fucking!" Or at least this is what the finished product is to look like. Now, Shirley lies on the hotel bed in her bra and panties, flesh-toned—a color like peanut butter—watching her assistant, Heidi, and Yaheem, one of the most beautiful men she'd ever laid eyes on and her love interest from the music video—she'd handpicked him herself from a stack of headshots—each snort a line of coke. A few moments earlier, Heidi had offered to take a photograph of Shirley pouting in her lingerie—Shirley didn't ask if the photo had been posted to her Instagram, but if it was, she was sure that she would read about it later when, bored and lonely in the early hours of the morning, she Googled herself. She found it an odd thing when famous people said that they never searched for themselves in the depth of remembrance that was the Internet. How could someone not be interested in what was being said about them? The key was a detached curiosity; the key was not to let it turn you crazy. Shirley had mastered this long ago. It was only once in a while that she read something that left her sore, like an article published months ago in a well-known black publication that included her name in a list of black female entertainers who used their bodies to advance their careers, which the writer called *complicit racism.* "Since when is journalism putting words in people's mouth?" Shirley tweeted to the writer. But the writer had only responded coolly, asking Shirley if she would like to be interviewed for a follow-up story, and because the response had only deflated Shirley's desire for an online altercation, she became bored by the whole thing and what had been anger was now a distracted annoyance. Besides, she was preparing for a performance, and memorizing her dance routine was better use of her energy.

Cocaine was something Shirley had done every once in a while when life warranted an extra indulgence—the release of a new album, or after the Grammys. She was careful about overindulging. But the death of a singer whose life and career had been taken by addiction, a singer whom Shirley had admired from childhood, had frightened her away from hard drugs. Now she'd only smoke ganja. More than anything,

Shirley was afraid of dying in the limelight. She had too much pride to be anyone's cautionary tale. "I don't fuck with that," she said when Yaheem took the cocaine out of his bag and called her over to the coffee table. He had pouted and raised his hand to playfully flick his wrist at her. He was such a beautiful man. It was too bad he preferred men—this became clear when during a break from shooting he'd told Shirley that he was sure he'd seen the director on Grindr. Nevertheless, it was funny to think of the relationship rumors that would arise—funny also to think of how the rumors would be nurtured and encouraged before cameras for a short period of time, the attention it would bring both of them for several months, the gossip magazines having something new to report. And then there would be another man whose name would be linked with hers. Fame was a constant surprise to her, or maybe, she sometimes thought, it wasn't a surprise but instead was the kind of thing that someone like her never became used to. It was why for a long time she was so careful with her money. She never thought—never imagined—that her career would last for as long as it has.

Now that the coke is finished, Yaheem and Heidi are sharing stories about their sex lives.

"I'm done with faggots," Yaheem says. "The last one gave me gonorrhea."

"Ha!" Heidi says. "I wish that was my cutoff point. An ex-boyfriend gave me gonorrhea. That's how I found out he was cheating on me."

"Y'all are nasty," Shirley says from the bed, but really she is delighted by the conversation. She sits up, leaning on one arm to look at Yaheem and Heidi, who are still sitting on the rug by the coffee table even though there is a blue velvet sofa a few feet away.

"What's the worst thing a boyfriend ever gave you?" Yaheem asks, and it strikes Shirley again that he is such a handsome man—one of those biracial types, the kind who people believe take the best from both races.

"Trouble," she says.

"That's boring," Yaheem says. "Every boyfriend gives trouble. I hate all of my ex-boyfriends. Tell us something juicier."

The truth is that the worst thing was a baby but it could have also been the best thing if both the timing and the man hadn't been so far from ideal. When Shirley thinks about carrying Huzzah the Rapper's child, she thinks about a baby who would have looked like him, a little girl with thick curly hair and a mouth too pink and pretty to belong to a man. But she couldn't speak honestly because Yaheem wasn't in her inner circle, and moreover, she couldn't tell how trustworthy he was, how quickly he would gossip to a magazine. And besides, Heidi was the kind of white woman Shirley didn't trust. White people who took themselves too seriously made her nervous.

"Chicken pox," she says finally. "When I was a little girl, the boy next door gave me chicken pox." It was true: the boy next door had given her chicken pox—there was still a faded scar on her forehead that makeup artists sometimes asked about as they smoothened the area with extra foundation coverage.

"I had no idea," Yaheem says slowly and dramatically, "that you would be so boring in person."

What could Shirley do but laugh? Sometimes, it fascinated her to think that so many people didn't realize that fame, the ability to be seen and seen and then seen some more, was in itself a performance. And if people were looking and talking, why not make the performance good? In interviews she could be candid, in pictorials sexually liberated, and the images that went along with her already provocative song lyrics pushed farther and farther the longer she was in the industry, as it was the only way to compete with the other pop stars. And a part of her really liked the drama of performing a persona—a part of her enjoyed the attention. Recently, on the cover of a gossip magazine, the headline had been "Is Shirley Having an Affair with a Married Man?" alongside a photograph of Shirley and an actor embracing on a New York street. The man's wife had been sipping coffee close by and had not made it into the photograph. Shirley had laughed long and loud when she saw the cover, which a friend texted to her, and she had told her assistant to go out and find her a copy. Heidi, prone to overdoing every task assigned to her, brought back several copies.

"What are you doing tonight?" Yaheem asks Shirley, looking pleased that he made her laugh.

"Her stylist and nail designer are coming tonight," Heidi says.

"Why? You want to go somewhere with me?" Shirley asks, winking at him.

"You should come to a gay club with me," Yaheem says.

"I would love that! I love gay men—"

"And they love you."

"But I have my period. Or I'm going to get it. I can feel that it's coming."

"Which is why you're lying on white sheets in lingerie."

"Tell me something, are you a top or a bottom?" Shirley has this game she likes to play with people; the only rule is that she asks intrusive questions. She's been playing it for a few years now—at first it had been a way to test her power, to see if people would deny her, and over time it became a way of asserting her power. Whenever someone put her in her place, she found herself drawn to the person. The women she wanted to befriend and the men she found herself attracted to. It hadn't happened this way with Huzzah the Rapper, but she'd wanted him anyway. He'd worn a superhero Halloween costume one time and the magazines had talked about the large outline of his penis. When Shirley met him for the first time, she'd asked, "Is it true that you have a big penis?" He'd laughed and lowered his head, and this, the fact that he could be shy, had charmed her.

"I'm whatever you want me to be," Yaheem says now, batting his lashes.

"Nasty."

"If that's what you want me to be," he says, giving Shirley an exaggerated pout.

• • •

"What's his last name?" Yaheem says to Heidi, jumping up off the floor. "What's his name?!" He's laughing, excited. He starts doing a silly little dance where he's swinging his arms from side to side and knocking his knees together.

"I can't remember!" Heidi says, laughing.

"Think!" he says, shaking her gently.

"It was so long ago!"

"This is important! Dig into the recesses of your brain."

"What are you two talking about?" Shirley asks, turning her attention from the several text message conversations she was having. One of the people she was texting is a rapper she sometimes flirts with—last year, the video they shot for their collaboration was steamy and seemed to have inspired hookup aspirations on his end. She enjoyed the attention, but unbeknownst to him, she'd sworn off rappers and hadn't recovered in a way where she could trust any man.

Yaheem falls to the floor, clutching his knees to his chest, and all the while laughing.

"We think we might have slept with the same guy," Heidi explains.

"She was talking about some redheaded guy she fucked who liked to lick cocaine off her feet and I was like, wait, I fucked a redheaded guy who licked cocaine off my feet. What are the odds, right? It has to be the same guy!" Yaheem sits up, wiping the tears from his eyes.

"I start to cry too when I laugh hard," Shirley says, smiling and shaking her head.

"Pleased to have something in common with you," Yaheem says, bowing his head.

"I had no idea you're such a freak?" Shirley asks, looking at Heidi with renewed interest.

"Eh, a little," she says, shrugging in a way that reveals that she is enjoying the attention.

"I looked at her and knew she was a freak," Yaheem says. It is becoming clear to Shirley that he can't stand not being the center of attention; perhaps a hyped romance before the paparazzi cameras was a bad idea. "I saw her glasses and high-heeled Mary Janes," he continues, looking at his nails and frowning, "and I knew that she liked to get her life. I'm not mad at that!" They all laugh, and he continues pestering Heidi to remember the redhead's name.

By the time Shirley climbs down from the bed and opens the bathroom door, Yaheem is tickling Heidi's belly. "I'm going to tickle you until you remember," he says. The last thing Shirley hears before the door muffles their voices is Heidi's laughter between words that spill out of her mouth: "They say that redheads are becoming extinct! It has to be the same guy." When Shirley pulls down her panties and sits on the toilet seat, it isn't until the coldness of the seat starts to wear away that she realizes that she's envious of the easy friendship between Yaheem and Heidi. During the video shoot, they'd gone on a smoke break together and those moments, short as they were, cemented something between them, and now the redhead was another thing they shared. Shirley has come to believe that Heidi is an opportunist—she has a way of weaving herself into the drama at hand, whether it is drugs, alcohol, or a juicy confessional by a young film star looking for sympathy in the bathroom of an exclusive nightclub on a Saturday night. And more annoying to Shirley, Heidi has a way of conquering people, connecting with them—even and especially famous people who have reason to be mistrusting of a bright hello from a stranger.

It isn't until Shirley grabs at some toilet paper to wipe that she notices that the seat of her panties is spotted with blood that is more brown than red—the usual way her body announces the first day of her period. Hissing her teeth, she pulls a tampon out of the bottom cupboard, annoyed that her period has come now, that it didn't hold off for a little while longer, because in two days she's performing for an awards ceremony in high heels and a white body suit. Shirley eases the tampon in, and, feeling that her bladder isn't quite empty, she sits back down on the toilet seat. A little liquid leaves, but when Shirley stands again, there is once again that unfinished feeling. She reasons that it could be a phantom thing—the brain not yet catching up to the body. She considers that it could be similar to how she can eat and eat in wait of that intuitive feeling of enough but when the brain finally catches up, she has already moved past enough to too much.

If life hadn't called her to singing, Shirley believes that she might have become a scientist. Lala, her hairdresser, laughs at Shirley's copies of *National Geographic* magazine and calls her a cornball, but when Shirley is turning the pages, running her fingers over photographs of animals, landscapes, and people, Lala will ask her to turn back so he too can admire. Late at night, especially after she's smoked a little weed while listening to reggae music, Shirley wonders about destiny—if such a thing exists, and if one could have had a different one if only for a different turn in life. Maybe whatever happens to someone is her destiny. If she never met Anthony Star at the resort and sang for him, if she never worked at the resort that summer, if her aunt never told her about the job—it astonishes her to think how easy it could have been to live a small life in a small place. Maybe, she sometimes decides, destiny is as flexible as a woman deciding what to wear on a given day.

Now, looking in the mirror as she washes her hands, Shirley turns her face from side to side—there is a burgeoning pimple on her chin, that's all. Her nose had been her former stylist's idea, and her makeup artist at the time, never mind the fact that he and the stylist were fucking, had agreed as though it was an obvious solution he had somehow over-looked the whole time he knew her. Everyone talked about how beautiful she would feel—subtle, but it would make a huge difference, they said. The few people who knew sent flowers after the surgery, but no one warned Shirley about how raw she would feel afterwards, as though someone could look at her new nose and take every secret thing, all of her insecurities, from where they were deeply buried. It felt like such an invasion, and one personally inflicted, which made her pain all the more confusing. The voices that spoke as though they knew better—the makeup and hair people and the music executives—told her, *Everyone does it.* They asked her, *You think so-and-so was born that way?* And in a way, they had been right: Shirley's career began to escalate in a way that mattered, her name and her face and the sound of her voice carrying into American households.

Afterwards, her first time back to Jamaica, Shirley had been nervous. In life, then and now, she is only afraid of one person. As soon as she walked through the door, her mother paused the show she was watching to take a long look at her daughter before asking, "Why yuh trouble yuh nose?" Later Diane would ask, with pity in her voice, "Who tell yuh fi trouble yuh nose?" It was as though her mother's questions gave Shirley the permission she needed to truly regret. She'd never imagined, though she could see what people meant when they said that she'd become more beautiful, that her nose had meant so much to her. It was, after all, only a nose. But it had been hers. It was the same nose that the women on her mother's side carried.

"Wha' happen to yuh nose?"

"Nothing. Nothing happened to it."

"Yuh going fi look inna mi face an' lie to me like seh mi ah idiot?" Diane shook her head at her daughter, and for a few moments looked deep in thought as though she was trying to remember something. Finally, she turned from Shirley and her nose, and returned to the forensic psychology show she had been watching.

When Shirley opens the bathroom door, she sees energetic hands, tongues, and Yaheem and Heidi hurriedly pulling apart. She is too tired, bored, and repulsed to ask the obvious questions. "No wonder you two were so quiet," she says, before reclosing the bathroom door and sitting back down on the toilet seat. Could she fire Heidi for this? Technically, she hadn't done anything wrong. If Shirley was honest with herself, she would admit that she never liked her assistant. From the way Heidi shook her hand the first day, it was obvious that she would take her job too seriously. She acted as though she was curing cancer or saving babies or doing something much more profound than assisting a pop star. She wore stylish frames and fashionable vintage clothes, but her face was pale and plain and the red lipstick she wore daily only ended up looking too harsh against her skin tone, revealing the imposter she was, a girl from a Midwestern farming town who moved to New York. They had this in common—the both of them from places important to those who inhabited them, less so for those who had moved away, and beyond the stretches of the imagination for those with other places on their minds. Shirley had considered this commonality whenever she overheard Heidi talking in an exasperated way about her hometown. Whenever anyone asked Heidi where she was from, she told them and then she would say, "But I've been in New York for thirteen years," as if that was all that mattered.

The job used to belong to Kerry-Ann, one of Shirley's childhood friends from back home. They were sometimes photographed in matching outfits—the both of them in high heels and that season's shade of lipstick. Shirley had industry friends but genuine intimacy and a shared history were harder to find, and so she clung to old friends. When it was revealed that Kerry-Ann had been stealing Shirley's clothes and selling them, she looked the other way for as long as she could. When Kerry-Ann started taking jewelry, there was a confrontation. At the end, it wasn't the stealing that had broken Shirley's heart but that her best friend wouldn't admit to what she'd done. Shirley had one of her security guards trail Kerry-Ann to a high-end secondhand store because otherwise she wanted to doubt that her friend was capable of stealing from her one moment and smiling into her face the next. It wasn't about the clothes and jewelry. They'd fought, told each other how they really felt. Kerry-Ann said that Shirley treated her as though she was her servant. "What the fuck do you think I'm paying you for?" Shirley had asked. "Do you think I'm paying you to be my friend?" That was four months ago and they hadn't spoken since.

Ten minutes later, when Shirley reopens the bathroom door, both Yaheem and Heidi are gone. She runs her eyes over the loftlike room, a temporary living space since her own place is being renovated, as though there is anywhere for them to hide. There are white floral arrangements on tables, high windows revealing a New York City skyline that looks like a postcard, and designer clothes lying in puddles on the floor. After a long day on set, this aloneness is a relief to her. She hopes that they don't come back from wherever they've gone to. Shirley plops back onto the bed. She picks up her phone from where she'd left it on the bed. The rapper wants to come over. She ignores him.

Now asleep, she is still wearing the purple extensions—

waist-long, a color vibrant and living, the shade of purple like the inside of a star apple from back home. Recently, in a documentary about the sea, Shirley had seen purple coral, and she'd been surprised that such a thing of beauty existed at the bottom of the ocean. Water frightened her—when it was deep and stretched far. When she was a little girl, there was a river close to where she lived. There was a day when Shirley swam too far out into the river. The water was above her head before someone pulled her out. For a long time afterwards, her mother would say that it was God why Shirley survived. Diane had brought up the almost drowning recently. Shirley had posed nearly naked for another magazine and Diane had called to put her daughter in her place, finally telling her, "Yuh neva drown dat day fi ah reason. I don't see why yuh can't sell music wid yuh clothes on."

What her mother didn't understand and what Shirley couldn't explain because it would reveal the slackness of her thinking, how far she really had come, was that she found that she could get used to plenty of things, including feeling comfortable, even bored, with her own nudity. At first, when the industry had been new, when the people in charge wanted her ass and her breasts to do what the music couldn't, she feigned comfort with her sexuality. Diane thought that Shirley should do a gospel album. It had seemed such a random suggestion until Shirley remembered that when she was a little girl she had wanted to use her voice to lead people to Christ. Now, it was a dream that seemed a lifetime ago and so well meaning that it might as well belong to another dreame

In a few days, Shirley would take time off to go to Ja

maica, the only place in the world where she could truly
relax. Everywhere else, whether she was sipping a beer in a
bikini on a yacht in St. Tropez or dipping out of a club in the
early hours of a New York morning with a rumored new
boyfriend, someone could snap a photograph of her, and the
moment would be taken from her and turned into something
other than what it was. Jamaica was the place she went to feel
unburdened. Maybe because it was the only place she ever
felt as though she truly belonged. She would stay in the big
house she had bought for her mother in a neighborhood
where wealthy islanders lived and foreigners kept vacation
homes. Diane would cook meals for her, all of her favorite
things to eat, and she would care for her only daughter, baby-
ing her and reminding her not to allow fame to turn her mad.
It hadn't all been recognition, awards, and money made.
There was the high-profile, tumultuous, and at the end dangerous relationship with Huzzah the Rapper—the relationship had nearly broken Shirley, and the whole world had
seen the bruises on her face. The image was reprinted again
and again as though it was something the world needed to
be reminded of. There was the period of time when Shirley
regularly got high. There was the abortion that had to be
had. And there was that surgery that made her more beautiful. Most of what happens to Shirley is unknown to her
mother. It comes to Diane not in details but in a foggy sense
of knowing, a shadow of everything her daughter has lived—
the way a mother intuits her child is lying but may not know
the reason for the lie or what the truth is. Nevertheless, Shirley's career, the highs and lows of fame, have been far better

and far worse than both mother and daughter could have hoped for. Shirley is only twenty-seven.

Part 2

The first day back home, Shirley lies in bed, sometimes sleeping and other times just lying there, rubbing the whole business in her mind so that every detail remains shiny. Finally, when the day is coming to a close, Diane demands that her daughter sit up and eat the dinner that she has prepared for her: chicken foot soup, Shirley's favorite. She sits up and takes the bowl from her mother, and realizes for the first time today that she is hungry. It seems that she hasn't been so hungry in a long time. She looks down at the thick soup for a long moment—yam, dumplings, and chicken feet swimming in a pumpkin broth.

"Something wrong wid di soup?" Diane asks.

"Nothing, Mommy," Shirley says, and then before another wave of hunger can hit her, she eats so quickly that the soup burns her tongue.

"Di soup taste good, Mommy."

"Yuh like di yellow yam? Di helper find ah nice piece ah di market day 'fore yestideh. I use di rest ah it inna di soup."

"Mi love it. Mi nuh know when last mi eat chicken foot soup."

"Why yuh nuh have di 'oman who cook for yuh mek it? Yuh paying her plenty ah money—yuh can tell her what fi cook. What she cook give yuh? White people food?"

"Mi nuh want anyone but you or some other Jamaican

cook Jamaican food fi me. Waste of time to put up wid di disappointment. One time I was craving curry chicken and rice and peas and I told Meghan to mek it fi me. I mek sure to tell her to make it Jamaican-style because one time I ordered jerk chicken at this expensive restaurant in Manhattan and it taste like dem fling some jerk sauce pon di chicken and call it jerk chicken. Mi couldn't eat it. When Meghan bring di food, I saw that she put mango inna di curry chicken, and the rice and peas ah two separate dish. Mi almost bawl. Mi could only ask her, why she put mango inna di curry chicken?"

Diane laughs energetically, and Shirley laughs with her, though less impressed by the old joke. It isn't the first time that Diane has heard about the chef's failures to cook satisfying Jamaican food. It pleases her that she can still provide for her daughter in this way—that even now after all the money Shirley has made, there is still this opportunity to care for her.

After Shirley finishes eating, Diane takes the bowl from her and watches as she crawls back under the covers. She is petite—like a little girl under the covers. Even Diane is constantly surprised by how much larger and more womanly her daughter looks on television, in magazines, and even in person when she is all dressed up in her makeup and high heels. Oh, how it would surprise the millions of fans all over the world to see Shirley now—her weave a natty mess, her skin free of makeup and a few pimples sprouting here and there, lying in bed in her panties and a T-shirt as though anything is wrong, as though she isn't one of the most blessed people in the world. Diane briefly considers that it's possible that Shirley can't help a certain sadness—after all, Diane's own mother used to lie in bed sometimes when the world got to be too heavy, and it was said that her mother's mother did the same thing. The sadness is a family thing, it seems—somehow it had gone and skipped Diane and her sisters, all of them women who refuse to lie down on a problem. Shirley had told her mother that a man she knew was killed by a drug overdose, but further questions had revealed that Shirley had just met the man, had never been romantically involved with him and in fact he was gay, and so Diane didn't understand why her daughter was so affected by the whole thing, and whenever she broached the topic, Shirley didn't have much to say. Diane takes one more glance at the small figure under the covers, and for a moment has the desire to pull the sheets off her daughter and demand that she face life, and warn her too that she didn't come into success to become one of those miserable rich people. Instead, Diane leaves the room, closing the door a little harder than necessary.

"Satan is aftah you," Diane had said, and the words had seemed so true and so absurd that Shirley had wanted to cry. That night when Yaheem and Heidi snorted the cocaine, that night when Shirley came out of the bathroom to see that the both of them had left, Heidi had gone home and Yaheem had gone, according to what Shirley would find out later, to a gay club where he would go home with a man. Later, they would find several drugs in his system. He was so briefly known, only just coming up, that his death had come and gone quietly. Night after night when sleep betrayed Shirley in that city they say never sleeps, there was little information to be acquired from the Internet. One of the few places that covered Yaheem's death was a newspaper in Louisiana— a local newspaper in a town that Shirley had never heard of before. "Yaheem was the son of a minister and a school-teacher, who were shocked to learn about their son's lifestyle and drug use. He filmed a music video with pop singer Shirley but in light of his recent death it's unknown whether the music video will be released." Shirley had arranged for Heidi to send flowers to the funeral. She had wanted to go, had wanted to travel to that little town in Louisiana, but she was afraid to face the grieving relatives. How to own even a little slice of grief for a man she'd only known for a day? She wouldn't belong.

A shame that the biggest thing he was to do was the music video they filmed together and that could never be released now. Shirley had fought—somehow it seemed important for the world to see it—but the people above had refused. Pick another guy, they said. Film another video, they said. But Shirley didn't want another guy and she didn't want another video, and eventually the people above had asked her, "Weren't you supposed to take some time off?" Oh, she said, remembering, because she really had forgotten. It had been hard to leave for a place so much farther from where she'd last seen Yaheem. She wrote down a line in her journal, "I am being haunted by a man I barely know." Maybe the words would work in a song. Once in a while, she wrote down song lyrics for someday. She'd long wrestled with the idea of attempting to write her own music in an effort to become the kind of artist with a stronger hold on her career instead of the pop star robot she at times felt like.

"Satan is aftah you," Diane had said, and when her mother leaves the room holding the bowl with the bones from the chicken foot soup, Shirley begins to cry, gentle sobs that grow louder so that it feels as though her entire body is crying, and finally, she exhausts herself and falls back asleep.

Diane is addicted to crime documentary shows because American crimes disturb her in ways that beckon for her attention. Of course, Jamaicans could be violent—after all, it was said that the worst-behaving slaves were sent to Jamaica, which accounted for the island's high murder rates. But killings in Jamaica lacked the imagination of the white men and women Diane watched on the Investigation Discovery channel. White women stole babies and poisoned lovers for health insurance, and white men brought guns into schools and killed their wives for the love of another woman. When she was a little irrational, she feared that she would lose Shirley and her remains would be discovered in some lonely corner of New York City. Diane didn't doubt that Shirley surrounded herself with questionable characters, and now that she and Kerry-Ann were no longer talking, there was no one she trusted to protect her daughter.

Even now, eleven years later, Diane wonders if she should regret sending Shirley, then sixteen, to America, where a music career was promised to her. The promises had been kept, more than kept, as it became evident that Shirley's potential for stardom was more than anyone thought it to be. But what had been lost? What kind of mother allows her daughter to leave at such a vulnerable age? Who had wanted fame more—Shirley or herself? It was a question she was always asking herself. Because if she had wanted it less, could she have sent Shirley away?

When Shirley enters the living room and sits next to her mother, she pulls some of the thin blanket her mother is using onto her own legs in the easy way of two people accustomed to sharing. Shirley had never quite understood why her mother never married or had more children—how sad that she watched so much gruesome television by herself.

"Yuh done sleep?" Diane asks, looking at her daughter only briefly before she turns her attention back to the television.

"What's dis one about?"

"A couple say dem 'ave open relationship an' di husband get jealous an' kill di wife other man."

"Wow," Shirley said, looking with surprise at the photograph of the couple because the man looks like he might wear khaki pants to work and the wife has a haircut reminiscent of a suburban mother.

"Tell me 'bout it. Di husband ask her fi stop see di other man and she continue fi see him. I neva understand why people can't understand dat wha' happen in di dark mus' come out in di light. It may tek a while but it a go 'appen. Always 'appen."

Shirley couldn't help feeling a little bit reprimanded. There was so much her mother didn't know. Ironically, the song that elevated her career, bringing her worldwide recognition, was the single "Don't Tell My Mother," from her third album, eight years ago. It was a reggae pop song that told the story of a young girl who wanted to do the kinds of natural, inevitable, and mildly dangerous things that call to young girls. *Ooh. Ooh.* Shirley had made rapturous eye contact with a boy who was really a man and danced in the music video in a bikini top and tiny denim shorts, the kind of clothing her mother would have never allowed her to leave the house wearing. But Diane had been in Jamaica when the music video was filmed, and later when she saw it and spoke to Shirley on the telephone, she had said, "Mi neva dream mi would see mi child pon TV like dat," but it had sounded like and unlike a reproach at the same time, as though her mother had already accepted with a dull reluctance the fact that fame came with expensive entry and maintenance fees. Shirley had been disappointed to be unchallenged.

"So when yuh an' Kerry-Ann going to mek up back?" Diane says, turning from the television now that the show is finished.

"Mi nuh know," says Shirley, already regretting this conversation and the fact that she didn't return to her bedroom after using the bathroom.

"Mi hear seh she's living wid a white man in Los Angeles," Diane says.

"Who tell you dat?"

"Her mother."

"Mi know she in Los Angeles but I didn't know she a live wid a man."

"Wha'? Yuh jealous?"

"Mi jealous? No. Why yuh ask me dat?" Shirley is rising. It frustrated her that her mother could assume the worst.

"No reason. I know seh you an' her were like sisters an' even fava each other an' mi trying fi think of what could ah come between you two."

Shirley hadn't told her mother about the stealing because she knew her mother would tell Kerry-Ann's mother, and ultimately she wanted to spare Kerry-Ann that indignity.

"Sit back down," Diane says. "Yuh know you too miserable? Fram when you likkle pickney yuh miserable. Memba when mi use to call yuh old lady?"

Shirley sits back down and can't help smiling. "Mi wasn't miserable. I was spoiled. Yuh bring it upon yuhself by spoiling me."

"Is not me who spoil yuh. Ah yuh fadah. 'Im neva like fi hear yuh cry."

Shirley's father had left Jamaica when she was still a little girl. He'd moved to Canada, where he had family living, and though he had promised to send for Diane and Shirley, they heard less and less of him until it was evident that he had carried on with a life without them. When Shirley's first album came out, he'd gotten in touch with Diane and she had listened for several minutes while he talked excitedly about Shirley and then she had told him never to contact her again. When she told Shirley about the phone call, she'd called him and was disappointed to realize that the man who she counted as a father was only a fan. "You should come to Canada and meet your stepbrother and stepsister," he'd said, and Shirley had wanted to cry at how casually he treated her, this man who when she was little hadn't liked hearing her cry. Even more hurtful, he never apologized for leaving her and her mother behind without so much as an explanation. He never even brought it up. After that, Shirley refused his phone calls, which was what her mother had been advising in the first place.

"I don't want Kerry-Ann fi live wid a man because dats who can tek care of her," Diane says, scrolling through the channels. "It's not ah good thing when ah young girl ha fi depend pon a man. Why yuh don't mek up back wid her an' give her back her job? You two been friends before di two ah you could even talk properly. You should mek up back wid her an' give her back her job."

Shirley doesn't respond, a desperate tactic she has learned to use with her mother. It wouldn't bother her if Diane simply asked for favors for herself and others, but instead she has a pressuring, subtle way of tapping into her mother role by telling her daughter what she should do. Shirley hates this—hates that her mother has the capacity to make her feel like a child, and that she behaves as though Shirley's money is their money. She'd started the silent treatment in the last year after her mother told her to hire a distant cousin as her housekeeper and the cousin had refused to work but expected to be paid, and firing her was a series of unnecessary dramas. Later Shirley found out that she and the girl weren't even biologically related.

Diane seems unfazed by her daughter's silence. She yawns and settles back into the Investigation Discovery channel. She's watching a show about a missing child who was taken as he walked home from a friend's house in a suburban neighborhood. Shirley is half watching the show and half wondering about Kerry-Ann, because who is this man she is living with? Of course he's a white man. Kerry-Ann loves white men. When Shirley teased her about the smaller penis size, Kerry-Ann said, "Jamaican men tink good sex is pushing a big dick into a woman. White men know how fi mek love. White men love fi eat pussy." The only man in recent memory Shirley could think of was a music executive who told Kerry-Ann he was separated from his wife after she slept with him. Shirley had called her a "Seventh-day Adventist slut" because Kerry-Ann was religious when she remembered to be, and they had laughed and reviewed the details of the hookup. It's only when Shirley hears light snoring that she realizes that her mother is asleep. She looks her mother over, noticing the professional manicure and pedicure, the neatly arched eyebrows, and the freshly relaxed hair that Diane would put into rollers before she climbed into bed.

As a child, Shirley had been protective of her mother's crossed eyes. Shirley had taken her beauty from her father— a light-skinned, green-eyed man with obvious European ancestry—and from her mother she had taken shapely thighs and a behind that was large enough to impress but small enough to fit into couture clothes. As a child, whenever any of her classmates brought up her mother's eyes, even if it was as innocent as "Is di lady wid di cross eyes yuh madda?" she would say, "Nuh chat 'bout mi madda like dat!" And because she had come to accept that her mother was the lady with the crossed eyes, she never imagined that her mother hadn't accepted herself. And so the request for the surgery came as a shock to Shirley. And afterwards, for a long time, whenever Shirley looked at her mother, it felt strange. It was like looking at the sky to see that something as eternal as the stars was no longer there. Shirley noticed other changes in her mother. She became more outspoken around Shirley's industry friends, and she put more effort into her outward appearance, wearing red lipstick for the first time in Shirley's life. She put a second hole in her ears. She wore a full face of makeup to go to the market. She traveled to New York more frequently to spend time with Shirley. She took more interest in the names of designers, the famous people Shirley partied with, and she started a Twitter account. Shirley watched, mildly entertained and horrified, and realized with a certain sadness that her mother was still a young woman, only forty-three, and had probably spent her whole life yearning to be beautiful.

When Diane wakes up, she sees Shirley's thin frame slipping out of the living room. Why was her daughter as thin as the white women on television? She had even lost her bottom. Diane would have to get some oxtail to make stew and some cow foot to make soup. The women in Diane's family, the ones on her mother's side, were known for their voluptuous figures—wide hips, round bottoms. Shirley had come like the women on her father's side who were thin and curvy in their own way without being as shapely and fat as her mother and her sisters. It was true that Shirley had a more ideal body for couture fashion and bikinis. It impressed, bewildered, and at times shamed Diane that she had given birth to and raised a daughter who was understood to be one of the sexiest, most beautiful women in the world. It would have made more sense if it looked like the apple, as they say, didn't fall far from the tree. Instead, it was that the apple, Shirley, was an entire other species of apple.

It had been a strange thing giving birth to a little girl so pretty. But in the days before anyone discovered that Shirley had a voice, her beauty was less intimidating. Some days it felt like a privilege, a blessing even, but on other days it was a thing a mother couldn't simply overlook without any resentment in her heart. A lesser woman than Diane would have taken it out on her daughter, but she had always loved her daughter. The envy was only a grating presence at the back of her mind, and one she was ashamed about. It had been strange getting attention from Shirley's red-skinned father. He was a neighborhood boy a few years older than she was, and he had been a friend of Diane's brothers. Growing up, he'd always paid her little mind until at sixteen he looked at her a long moment and she knew that she had him. He had been surprised that the sex was good, that Diane was such an enthusiastic participant and it was convenient sex, and so he had kept coming back until she discovered that she was pregnant. Shirley had been Rodney's first child, and the fact that there was a living artifact of himself in the world, and one so pretty, light-skinned and green-eyed like his mother, was why he stayed with Diane for the first five years of Shirley's life. Diane had known that during these years there had been other women, but Rodney had given her and their child the dignity of returning home to them in the evenings for dinner. Those days he worked for the meat man and he would come home with the fatigue of dealing with blood and bones all day. Those days he had said that he almost wanted to stop eating flesh except that he would miss it too much. He would come home and sit on the steps in front of his mother's house, which is where they all lived, and sitting on the steps he would hold Shirley in his lap and Diane had been very happy because it seemed that she'd made life. Here was the beautiful child, here was the man who told her he loved her, and what a surprise that it all belonged to her. She was only eighteen. At the time, as is sometimes the case with the very young, she'd wanted very little from life.

It always seemed to Diane that Shirley could sing. She was singing for as long as she was talking, and so the fact that Shirley could sing wasn't in itself a surprise to Diane. Her own mother sang and the only place it took her was to the church choir and to a man who enjoyed listening to her. The first time anyone made mention of Shirley's voice was when she was five. A woman who lived several houses down the road was passing by the house where Shirley stood at the edge of the grass driveway picking flowers off the hibiscus bush and singing one of the popular gospel songs from the radio. Diane was sitting on the steps in front of the house, shelling peas. The woman looked up at Diane for a long moment as though she had to find the words. "But she can sing?" she finally said. "Like a bird," Diane said, and hadn't thought much of it, until the next day the woman came back and asked if Shirley would sing the special selection in church that Sunday. Diane had been taken aback but she sent Shirley because she figured that nothing bad could come out of a little girl singing a song in a church. As more and more people were astonished by the quality of Shirley's voice, Diane came to be proud. Her daughter's talent gave her a sense of visibility that she had never had in her life. People stopped her on the street and asked her if she was Shirley's mother. All of this extra attention, and she started visualizing the day when people would look at her and her eyes wouldn't call attention to themselves. She encouraged Shirley to memorize songs and she coached her. By the time Shirley was ten, it seemed a week didn't go by without her singing in some church or another. By the time she was fourteen, she had nearly won an island-wide singing contest on television. An older woman won the competition but everyone knew that Shirley was cheated. When the music man finally showed up at the resort, the rest, as people say, was history.

Part 3

Shirley's belly full of cornmeal porridge and fried plantain with bread, breakfasts from her childhood, that other life, when she had been poor. Yet food satisfying all the same for reasons so complicated and nebulous and obvious that there is no encompassing language for it. Diane had brought a tray in, and nudged her daughter awake. Shirley drank the cornmeal porridge in bed, lying on her side, blowing at the first few spoonfuls. The plantain and bread she ate standing at her bedroom window looking down at the pool. She ate quickly, hungrily, having slept through the early hours of evening and throughout the night. She'd woken up at 4 a.m. to use the bathroom, and afterwards she had considered looking for something to eat but then sleep revisited her, and with it came a recurring dream: she's in a gay bar and she's moving through the packed space, looking for Yaheem. There are men everywhere—beautiful men, dancing ones, ones who have drunk too much and are kissing in corners—and they are all calling to her, touching her shoulders as she passes so that she will look their way. But she can't stop. She has to find Yaheem. That's all she can ever remember from the dream.

Looking down at the pool, Shirley counts on her fingers the hours she spent sleeping: fifteen. A week in Jamaica, and mostly all she's done is sleep. After the breakup with Huzzah the Rapper, there had been a period of time—a span of months that felt longer—during which it seemed that all she did was sleep. Shirley had no idea, and barely any recollection of, how she managed to record the album that came out the following year. When she finally awoke, regaining a more normalized sleeping routine and replacing sleep with weed and cocktails, she was fifteen pounds lighter, which her stylist, Bastian, a gay black man from the South who spoke in a

British accent, used to his advantage. It could be argued that it was Shirley who reintroduced the midriff from the nineties—but she wore it elegantly, not like those pop stars from back in the day who looked as though they were desperate for the easy attention their sexuality brought them. Girls like that pouted too obviously, no subtlety whatsoever, and they behaved as though they'd discovered sex, when in fact there wasn't anything new or interesting or even surprising about how they presented themselves. It was all more than a little boring. Now, after her seventh album, Shirley has developed a coolness about her sexuality—"Ain't no thang," she seems to be saying in pictorials and music videos. She is rock and roll and red lipstick and long extensions. She is eyeliner and cigarettes and tattoos. All of this, and in a pencil skirt and a pair of boots made for men, with her belly button hanging out. It's all more than a little bit clichéd but enlivened with the understanding that she's an exotic, sun-kissed specimen from an island paradise, and in this way, she isn't another Madonna-esque pop star. The magazines notice. Fashion designers notice. Shirley holds the world's stare, or at least she dares herself to. Last year, one magazine dubbed her "The Most Beautiful Woman in the World." Another one dubbed her "The Sexiest Woman Alive." She is regularly featured in celebrity Best Body pictorials, and because in interviews she could never confess the truth, that she'd gotten her body because she'd been depressed and had somehow never been able to regain those fifteen pounds, she talks about lean protein, green juice, and an exercise routine with a celebrity trainer. This, after all, is an appropriate response and, moreover, the kind of thing people expect to hear.

There is a feeling that this day holds more possibility than the previous ones, where sleep held her in its arms so tightly and so tenderly that there was little effort to untangle from it. Maybe, Shirley thinks, God has finally answered her prayers. Or perhaps the meal invigorated her. The decision to change into a bikini isn't a conscious one. Shirley sits at the edge of the pool, massaging her belly, admiring the fullness. A strand of wind comes to her, and with it a memory. When she was a little girl, the white children on television ate spaghetti with tomato sauce. What it tasted like Shirley hadn't a clue, but because the white children on television desired this meal, she came to desire it too. There was a time when she decided that this meal that she hadn't had in her life was her favorite thing to eat. Oh, how she cried whenever her mother put cornmeal porridge or boiled yams, green bananas, and dumplings in front of her. "You nuh see you too mawga?" Diane would say as tears slipped down Shirley's face, because she wasn't allowed to leave the table until she'd eaten a substantial amount off the plate. There was a time a relative living in the United States sent a barrel to Jamaica, and the food, clothing, and household items were parsed out amongst the family members. Included in Diane's share were two packages of spaghetti and two jars of tomato sauce, and when Shirley saw this, she jumped up and down. Shirley was nine years old at the time, old enough to boil water herself, and so she cooked the spaghetti by following the directions on the package carefully. When it was ready, it met Shirley's expectations—it was indeed after all her favorite thing to eat. She twirled the spaghetti on her fork, imitating the white children on the television. Diane, however, took one bite, screwed up her face, and dismissed the whole business as "white people food." Shirley paid her mother no mind—she had long mistrusted her mother's taste in food. This was after all a woman who delighted in eating tripe with boiled green bananas and cow foot soup. Shirley ate a large share of spaghetti, half the package, and because of the heaviness of the meal, sleep came without her realizing.

The next morning, she learned that her mother had packaged the rest of the spaghetti to be taken to school for lunch. And how excited Shirley was to show her friends the spaghetti, to tell them how it came all the way from America. Of course, when they begged, she would share a little, and when they asked for more, she would share a little more but not too much because it was her lunch. In the hours before lunch, she told her friends about the spaghetti but to her disappointment they were only mildly interested. Maybe, she thought, her friends weren't more excited because they had to see what she meant. Maybe they didn't understand. Maybe they didn't believe her. When it was finally time to eat, she went to her desk but when she opened up the plastic container she saw that there was a large cockroach sitting in the spaghetti and tomato sauce. She almost wanted to cry. She put the container back in her desk and she didn't eat lunch that day. She didn't have any money and home was too far away to walk to. While playing outside with her friends, one of them asked about the spaghetti, but to Shirley's relief another friend said something else and so the moment passed. Later at home, Shirley was angry and humiliated and she asked her mother about the cockroach in a tone that sounded like an accusation—what she wanted to know was, *How could you let this happen to me?* But since she was a child, since she only had the language of childhood, she whined.

Since the cockroach was still lying dead in the spaghetti and tomato sauce, Shirley showed it to her mother, but Diane had the wrong response—she laughed. This exacerbated Shirley's desire to cry. Diane stopped laughing long enough to reveal that she didn't know how the cockroach got into Shirley's lunch. Perhaps, she explained, the cockroach climbed in as she transferred the spaghetti from the pot to Shirley's lunch container the night before school. It was an unsavory thing to happen to a little girl. Shirley knew that those little white children on television didn't open their lunch boxes to find cockroaches. She lost interest in spaghetti after that—the remaining box of pasta and the jar of tomato sauce sat idly on a shelf until a few months later when there was nothing else to eat in the house. Diane ate the spaghetti because she could do no better, and after examining that there were no cockroaches on her plate, Shirley twirled the spaghetti with the joy and determination of reacquainting oneself with an old lover. She ate her share as well as what was left on her mother's plate. *Why this memory,* Shirley asks herself, *and why now?* She remembers herself, her toes dipped into the water, her nipples sensitive against her bikini top—her period must be on its way.

In the beginning, it felt weird and surprising to come home to Jamaica to a house that wasn't the home she'd known all her life. The large spacious rooms and new furniture felt like an unwelcome stranger pulling her into a hug. Now, Shirley is more comfortable with the fact that most things in her life are new, and in this way absent of the history that comes from being passed down and reused again and again in the way of the poor. But once in a while something will trigger a memory from the time when she was just Shirley from a small place. It happened days ago, when the chicken foot soup burned her tongue and she remembered being a little girl at the house where they used to live. There'd been a time when the soup burned her tongue and her mother put a cup of water in her hand. There was nothing profound about the memory—just a little piece of childhood come back to haunt her. She'd moved her mother out of that house with the old chicken coop in back and the crumbling steps in front, and bought her a home in a wealthy neighborhood. It had been the right thing to do, the safe thing to do.

But the house had been a lonely place for Diane. The neighbors were lawyers and doctors and foreigners with homes abroad—none of them the kind of country people Diane took a natural liking to, because the truth is that such people, the educated kind, intimidated her. When Diane wasn't speaking to old friends on the telephone, she was welcoming her sisters and other relatives into her home with its too many rooms. It was the only way she could navigate the wide, white rooms of the house.

A pool in Jamaica makes little sense to Shirley, as it is a

poor comparison to the sea. The sea, that culmination of land and sky, that blue a color living and holy, a color that can be heard and seen, smelled and felt, a color that can also be tasted. For Shirley, pools made more sense in the States, made sense because of those weak excuses Americans called beaches. Now, she decides that she feels like swimming and today the pool will suffice. A strand of thought from somewhere deep, and Shirley decides—and this realization comes to her slowly—to be happy. Yes, she will be happy. She is a famous singer and beautiful to more than a few people— both childhood dreams come true. There are no cockroaches. There is no reason to be anything other than happy. Meanwhile, behind her, through the kitchen window, Diane peels carrots for the cow foot soup and looks at her daughter's narrow back, the pale pink bikini, the flawless brown skin, watching, admiring and apprehensive, and contemplating what is to become of Shirley in the same way one might listen carefully to hear the note that signals the end of a song.

ACKNOWLEDGMENTS

I believe in the old-time wisdom that a village raises a child, and this is certainly true for a book that rises up from infancy.

Thank you, Amie Barrodale, for taking it upon yourself to introduce me to Jin Auh—you didn't have to do that. And thank you, Jin, for believing in my stories and for working on my behalf—two incredible gifts I don't take for granted. My appreciation to Luke Ingram for representing my writing in the U.K., and to everyone else in my corner at the Wylie agency. Andra Miller, I am forever grateful for your care with my work. I so appreciate you and your editorial genius. Kris Doyle, thank you for your enthusiasm and your vision, and for everything you've done to bring this book to the U.K.

My gratitude to the teams at Ballantine and Picador for having my back, and for everything they've done to bring this book into the world.

I am indebted for tremendous support from the Iowa Writers' Workshop. Thank you to my kind, inspiring writing instructors—Marilynne Robinson, Ayana Mathis, Ethan Canin, Daniel Orozco, Geronimo Johnson, and program visionary, Lan Samantha Chang. Thank you Connie Brothers, Kelly Smith, Deb West, and Jan Zenisek, for all you do to keep Dey House running. Readers and friends, and further evidence that Iowa City is a treasured place for a writer to find herself—Elizabeth Weiss, Brian Booker, Jake Hooker, Clare Jones, Rebekah Frumkin, Yaa Gyasi, Tom Corcoran, Tom Quach, Christa Fraser, Okwiri Oduor, Novuyo Rosa Tshuma, Aamina Ahmad and family, and Okezie Nwoka. Riley Johnson, thank you for reading the first draft of this book, and for being one of the best men I know. Nana Nkweti, your kindness and brilliance have been an example to me. Love to Naomi Jackson and Stephen Narain, classmates and Caribbean kinfolk, for welcoming me so lovingly to Iowa City. Jorge Guerra Del Cid, Iowa City feels like a map of our friendship, and you have been a home for me.

Thank you to the Whited family for support, and Troy Bond at Lucky's and Jason Paulios at the Iowa City public library for part-time jobs. Stephen Lovely, the director of the Iowa Young Writers' Studio, might be the most compassionate person to work for.

And thank you to the staff at *The Paris Review* for their editorial wisdom and kindness.

Friends, readers, and co-workers—Ransom Woodson, Heidi Kuchta, Kia Lindsey, Ruben Lebron Villegas, Meghan Metier, Tyler Tritten, Helen Rubinstein, Kaylia Duncan, Pauline Remy, Aracely Mondragon, and Miguel Torres. Faith Avery and La'Kesha Manning, thank you for the camera and for everything else.

For everyone who shared words, laughs, and meals while I was working on book edits in Mexico City.

For everyone who listened, soothed, and inspired, all the days of my life.

Love to my women friends—Melissa Apedo, Salisa Hudson, Joy Hibbler, Linda Diga, and Itisha Jefferson.

Donald Arthurs, I haven't forgotten how you used to tell us stories from your childhood, and that you brought those beautiful picture books from the city.

Love to my aunts, uncles, cousins, and my sweet nephews, Joshua and Jonathan.

To my family—my mother, Veronica Arthurs, and my siblings, Amanda Arthurs and Allan Arthurs. I am always thinking of you three.

ALEXIA ARTHURS was born and raised in Jamaica and moved with her family to Brooklyn when she was twelve. A graduate of Hunter College and the Iowa Writers' Workshop, she has been published in *Granta*, *The Sewanee Review*, *Small Axe*, *Virginia Quarterly Review*, *Vice*, and *The Paris Review*, which awarded her the Plimpton Prize in 2017.

Twitter: @AlexiaArthurs
Instagram: @alexiaarthurs